Shattered Heart
The Charli Jensen Story

Carol May

Book 1
Life's Second Chances Series

Dedication

This book is dedicated to my Mother, Sue Maynard, who has always supported me in all my crazy endeavors. Thank you for giving me the love of reading and a passion for books at an early age. You have shown me how to be a strong, caring, confident, intelligent woman with dignity. Because of this and all the other strengths you nurtured in me over the years, I found the courage for Charli Jensen to be born.

Chapter 1

This is the day that I have spent the last ten years fantasizing about. Most women dream of love, weddings, and children. Been there, done that except for the child part. I don't ever intend on going back there. Long term relationships are not for me. Nope! Not me! I have had my sights set on something completely different. The way I imagined I would feel today was nothing compared to the actual bundle of nerves I am. The fantasy that began all those years ago is what kept me going, when what I really wanted to do was toss in the towel and say to hell with it. Standing in the corridor outside my apartment waiting for the elevator I can't help but smile as I think back to my teenage years. I can almost hear my Mama as if she is right here beside me. Anytime I wanted to toss in that proverbial towel, she would start with the speech. It's the one she would tailor to meet either mine or one of my brothers needs.

Mine always went something like this. "Listen to me, miss. I am not letting you quit. This world is difficult enough for women." This is about the time she would begin the whole index finger pointing at me with that look on her face that only a mother can have. "Never, and I do mean never, give up on your dreams no matter what they are. The best things are worth waiting for. Dig deep inside you, and use that inner strength I know you have. You can do this."

Sometimes she would throw in other inspirational quotes to jump start my confidence.

Even now it pains me to acknowledge she was so right. Many many times I've had to dig deep to find the wherewithal to continue. Take this day for example, who would have thought all those late night drink induced plans my college roommate and best friend, Lana and I made are actually taking life. Like most college girls, we dreamed of visiting far-away lands and maybe finding an exotic man or two along the way. Remembering those conversations and sheer willpower kept me going! My mother was right. I did have it in me to get through some really difficult situations. I just had to search within myself to find my strength to overcome the obstacle that laid in front of me.

Lord knows during these last few months, I've thought more than once about sending an email to all those people that said I would never succeed. The church version would simply say- in your face. I did it! However, I would never get past my Midwest upbringing, as Mama used to say, and actually click send. Writing it would be no problem. I've written it more than once. At one point, a banner hung above my door during rehab that held that same saying. Smiling, I admit that the thought of a picture on social media with me in front of the Miami Beach City Limits sign giving them the big middle finger hello might do the trick. Nope, can't do that either.

That girl isn't me. Hey, maybe I could just post a picture of our business, Supreme Corporate Travel, on several sites with the tag line, owner Charli Jensen. As much as I can dream about doing any or all of those things, deep down I know I am not the woman that would do any of them. However, I am the woman that is making a play for her first big business connection today.

As I step out of the elevator into the lobby, I realize I left my coffee sitting on the kitchen counter. Darn! With a shrug of my shoulders, I smile when I remember I don't have to worry about being five minutes late. I am not going to be reprimanded by some clock watching boss. With that pleasant little thought, I decide to stop at the coffee shop just around the corner from the office. Pondering the thought walking the five blocks from my apartment building, I will burn off a few extra calories can and definitely splurge on a large cup of my favorite morning pick me up. Shaking my head, who am I joking? I am not going to walk. Admittedly, I do need the additional exercise since it seems as if I have abandoned my gym membership but that line of thought is for another day. What the heck, I'll settle for a medium size cup and a taxi. Yep, that sounds better. My feet like the idea also since these shoes are not the most comfortable ones for walking the one block to the office much less five.

Closing the taxi door, I feel my phone vibrating. By the time I find it in my bag and drag it out, of course, it's stopped but I see it was from my business partner, Lana Lewis. I read the message and think, God this girl knows me so well. I quickly text back answers to her questions.

No, I didn't oversleep.

Yes, I am on my way.

Yes, I have the proposal that I polished up last night.

Left my cup of coffee so am stopping at The Java House.

Want anything?

Before I can lay my phone down it vibrates again

Sure, x-large cup of Terrance!

Smiling, I shake my head at her, as if she could see it. Terrance is the long, tall drink of water that Lana has been drooling over for the last few months.

Don't know why u don't just break down and ask him out. U know he is interested.

Almost without any pause she sends back to me, *I might if he doesn't get the hint soon.*

She makes no sense to me. How she can be so straight forward in a meeting but shy and almost awkward when it comes to approaching a man.

At, JH be there soon.

The sweet aroma of coffee takes over my senses as I push open the door. Looking around the cheerful room, what do I find as I step inside? A line. Not just a line but a really long one! Of all mornings for me to forget my coffee. Oh well, I suppose this just gives me another reason to appreciate being a small business owner. If we can land this account today hopefully we won't always be the smallest executive travel company. Maybe, if I get Rose's attention, she can go ahead and make my cup. It's not like I ever change orders. Scanning the room one more time, I decide that is wishful thinking. She'll never see me with these tall men ahead of me. Even with these four inch heels, I feel like the newest dwarf, Shorty. What is it open try outs for Miami's pro basketball team?

The line moves forward pulling me out of my haze which I am sure has been brought on by a lack of caffeine flowing through my system. I notice the man in front of me. Scanning his broad shoulders then allowing my eyes to move downward, the only thing I can think at this moment is, nice. Very nice! How could I have been standing behind this perfectly shaped specimen and just now be noticing him? Of course, the fact that he just put his hands in his pockets, helps with the sculpture I am so admiring. As my eyes travel down to his perfectly formed calves that represent hours in a gym, I have no doubt, I can't help but continuing to admire the view in front of me. If the rest of this human tree standing in front of me looks anything like the back, then yum.

I love living here! Where else but Miami can a woman find something this gorgeous on a daily basis. A great deal of the people here spend many hours in a gym to maintain their beach bodies, that's just not for me. I suppose I have always been lucky that I have a relatively high metabolism which allows me to burn off quite a few calories.

Closing my eyes I visualize him walking out into the Atlantic, the ripple of muscle moving across those bronzed broad shoulders. His wet swim trunks clinging to his perfectly shaped backside. Pausing in the waves, he raises his hand and runs his fingers through his hair. Oh, my! I must learn to control my thoughts because the rest of my body is beginning to join in on the admiration of this fine specimen in front of me. My breasts are the first to respond. Thank God, my bra is contoured which is providing my peaking nipples with enough camouflage that no one will be the wiser. Bringing myself out of this daydream, my conscience also wakes up. What in the world am I thinking? Tree? Did I actually describe this gloriously tall man as a tree?

Shaking my head I think to myself, you can take the girl out of the sport but not the sport out of the girl. Tree! I sound like I'm back at Mom and Dad's watching a basketball game with my brothers. Squeezing my eyes shut even tighter, I think of my

9

brothers. Crap! I do sound like them way back when all they talked about was a woman's looks. I hated the way they spent time ranking their dates based on looks and what they laughingly referred to as assets. It didn't matter if the girls had a brain or not. What mattered was that scale business. Scores from one to ten. Of course, those Walker boys never had anything under an eight even on a bad day, to hear them tell it. Thank goodness they can't hear me or I would catch all amounts of...

"Damn! Excuse me."

My eyes fly wide open as I realize Sexy Butt turned around with his coffee. Looking up into blue eyes, that rival the waters of the Caribbean all I can mutter is, "Is that my fault?" as I grimace and point to his chest.

Almost scornfully, I hear him say, "No darlin, not at all, I always make it a habit of spilling freshly brewed coffee down my shirt front! Whose fault do you think it is?" I look around frantically for something to hand him as I mutter out some stupid statement about napkins usually being here.

He continues on in his rumbling voice right over my words, "Thank God it was iced to help with this early heat or I would be burned. You should watch yourself. For God's sake, don't ever stand that close to someone in a coffee shop. Anyone with any brains at all knows that."

Speechless, I simply stand watching the way his shirt is clinging to his chest as napkins magically appear. He jerks them out of the mysterious hand and begins wiping down his front, my imagination provides a clue as to the ripple of his abs he is wiping down. The spill really isn't as bad as he claims. For just a minute I am lost in watching those large hands move at a rapid pace. Admittedly, I wouldn't mind if they moved over me.

Grimacing, the only response I can mange is actually pathetic, "I am so, so sorry. I must have been focusing on something else."

He barely grunts a response as I watch him storm off muttering something about getting back to his yacht to change. As he exits the building, I realize the other men are following him. Suddenly, the height of the customers has shrunk to what I would call average.

Stepping forward, I turn to the counter, "Hey Rose, I'll take my usual along with a side of what just walked out of here but can you just add a touch of personality?" I have no doubt that she can see the lust in my eyes. Oh crap, can she see my peaks? If she can does that mean he could? Crap! Double crap! I bet Rose can even read the imaginary neon sign above my head that is flashing needs sex, needs sex soon.

"I hear you girl. I'd take some of that anytime just as long as he kept his mouth shut. Hey do you think he would mind if I bound and gagged him?"

11

Using the old one finger pat on my chin pretending to be in deep thought, I casually ask, "Maybe, I should have offered to lick off any iced coffee that might have soaked through onto that broad chest. What do you think?"

With a light laugh, and a shake of her head, she says, "Girl, you are too much. You want the usual?" Turning away not waiting for my answer, she asks over her shoulder, "Will we see you and Lana at Billy's tonight?"

Shaking my head, "Not sure yet, sort of depends on my day. I think Lana has a date tonight" I say loud enough that anyone standing close might hear as I casually glance over at Terrance. I can't wait to tell her about the look he flashed my way when I threw out the date comment. She is going to be so happy. I sound like I am back in junior high, what in the world?

Houston Donovan

Walking down the steps, I find Nash in my kitchen with a mug of coffee to his lips. "Damn man, don't you have coffee at your place? Maybe, I should rethink you having keys to my homes."

Raising his mug up to me, "Not the good stuff." With a lift of his eyebrows Nash continues, "Houston, you know damn well that I need keys to all your homes." This is the only reply I get from the man standing in my kitchen who is continuing to drink my specially imported blend. Glancing over at one of my most trusted confidants, I half smile at him. "If a bag of Blue Island coffee placed in your kitchen is the only requirement to keep you satisfied, I'll contact the building staff that I so generously pay to ensure you have one."

"Pardon me asking but why would I want a bag? Our place doesn't have a service that comes in every morning to guarantee things are ready for me to eat" (as he picks up a fresh blueberry muffin) "or drink" (holding his mug up).

"Maybe you don't have that here but back in NYC, I know Cynthia does all that for you."

"Heck of it is Houston, I'm not in NYC, now am I?"

"Don't blame me, if the head of my security team chooses to come with me and leave that hot, sexy woman of his. I don't twist your arm Nash old buddy."

Turning to fill two travel mugs of coffee, and lifting his eyebrows Nash's reply drifts over his shoulder, "Do you have any idea how much shit I keep you out of on a daily no hourly basis? I can only imagine the firestorms you would bring back to me if I remained in the Big Apple."

Processing what Nash said, I flash back to college and the first problem he solved for me, one woman in my dorm room, another one knocking on my door. Laughing at the memory, I couldn't agree more with him. He definitely keeps a great deal of difficult situations at bay.

Looking at my watch, I ignore his last statement by saying, "Let's get going to this meeting. I have put the Miami office off for as long as I can. More than likely by the end of the day, the storms will have increased ten times after the ass chewing they are going to get."

Chapter 2

Charli Jensen

Walking toward my office, Lana stops me by saying, "It's about time you got here. Where have you been?"

My first thought is you are not my mother but I contain it. I really should expect questioning since I am late and after all today is a big day for us. Besides, I know high strung she can be. I admit, "I'm running a few minutes late but goodness it isn't the end of the world that I am not here when the door is unlocked. Lana, what is up with you? I told you in my text that I was stopping for some much needed caffeine. By the way, remind me to tell you about what happened at The Java House." Thinking back, I can't help but smile just a tad.

Continuing on in a tone that is uncharacteristic of her she says, "If you had read my other text you would   know that the meeting with The Blaine Company has been rescheduled by the "top dog" (I hate it when she uses air quotes) Mr. Blaine Carlton himself and by the way, "Who names their company after themselves using their first name? I can only imagine how big his ego is."

Clapping my hands, "Lana, focus! What about Mr. Carlton?" I ask her in my best I'm getting annoyed tone. In another minute I just might break into the toe pat that would definitely signify the level of irritation that I am reaching.

Shaking her head, just like the old days, to refocus. "Oh, yeah, anyway he arrived in town unexpectedly and has summonsed local office heads to an impromptu meeting on his yacht." Rolling her eyes as if she is offended in some way she continues, "with instructions to reschedule all meetings till next week. Can you believe that?"

In a somewhat mocking tone, I respond, "I know, pretty selfish, I agree. How dare he have a meeting on his yacht?" I nod my head in agreement continuing "but we both know if you're one of the wealthiest men in the United States you can do that. Snap your fingers and people juggle their lives to meet your needs."

Looking at me as if I have just spouted some type of prolific verse, Lana speaks in a sudden upbeat tone, "You're right, Charli. Let's view this as a sign. Our presentation/plan must need more work. Let's get busy adding those tweaks so we can take some of that money off his hands. Thanks for bringing me back to reality."

Smiling at my best friend, I say "Lana, that's what we do for each other. That's what true friends are for, balancing out each other's crazy." Laughing, my thoughts flash back to some of the stunts we pulled in college. If my parents ever found out some of that stuff, my butt would have been back in Kansas quicker than Dorothy ever dreamed of.

"Yep, we do but Lord help the world if our crazy happens at the same time." We slowly turn our heads and look at Joan. Then back at each other. "Joan, the duty will fall to you to bring us back to Earth if that ever happens." Smiling, Lana continues, "If that should ever happen we may have to find a way to give her a substantial raise."

Grimacing just a bit, I say, "Let's focus on the positive side of this meeting being postponed. What I can't believe is we are getting a chance to pitch for the Miami office's business to begin with. I must admit that what I read in my research giving small start up businesses a chance is one of the things The Blaine Company is known for."

Gently smacking my upper arm, I just know Lana is attempting to burst my bubble when she says, "Charli, aren't you jumping just a little ahead? Simply because we have the opportunity to present our idea for a company retreat doesn't mean we have the job."

"That small tidbit hasn't slipped my mind but we have to be positive. Positive Lana, positive. On that note, I'm off to drop the things in my office." After agreeing to get together to review the small changes I made last night, I leave them discussing a new client. Walking away, I casually toss out, "Since Mama Lana is watching, I'll be at my desk." Heading into my office, I think about how Joan was really a true find when we began the interview process. Sometimes, I know she was sent to us by a divine power. She really has balanced us out. I pray the next employee we add will fit in as well.

Since the meeting for this morning is rescheduled for next Tuesday, I can get ahead on other proposals I've put off along with tweaking some projects we have already secured. Who would have known that daydreaming about those tropical islands all those years ago would have led to a career for me.

I can't decide how our proposal was received. I know we were up against some other companies that can offer more but we can offer fantastic service with great detail to client needs. Our company is young but I really hoped to receive an acceptance today of our "upscale leisure travel" package. I can't wait to get out of this building and talk to Lana. It's killing me to find out how she feels about our meeting. I know her heart is racing as fast as mine. If I was five again, I would be jumping up and down with excitement. "Will this elevator never get here?" I push the button for the third time.

In the calmest voice I have ever heard come from Lana she declares almost as if she is scolding a small child, "Go ahead and do that again. We all know that will help it arrive faster."

"I sure hope you can read my mind right now, Lana." Elbowing her just a little, I continue as I face her, "Just in case you can't look deeply into my eyes and read between the lines, I will be more than happy to hold up my middle finger to share the gesture for my thoughts if that action is necessary?"

Without an opportunity for further conversation, due to the ding announcing the elevators arrival, I turn to wait patiently. However, when the doors open, I am a little concerned if we should attempt to squeeze into the already full car but before I can say we'll wait for the next one, Lana steps on causing all occupants to shift a little closer. Inhaling deeply I have little choice but to follow. Lana knows, I hate elevators in general but when they are this full, I feel almost claustrophobic. Standing here, we've morphed into one of the elevator zombies with our eyes focused on the panel beside the door as we descend, no one is speaking. I wonder if everyone feels as uncomfortable as I do about standing this close to complete strangers?

As we descend, I hear a man in the back say none to subtly, "I'm sorry sir had I known this elevator would have been so full, we could have taken the private one."

Attempting to keep my anger at bay, I inhale deeply and slowly exhale. Did I really just hear that man apologize to someone about this elevator being so crowded? In the words of my brother," you have

19

got to be f****** joking?" If they have access to a private elevator, why not use it? Why fraternize with the peons? Really! That just hits me the wrong way. I feel Lana's hand slowly slide onto my wrist and squeeze. She knows just how that rude comment is pushing me close to the edge. How does she always know? I understand this is her saying, keep with the breathing technique, let it go. Glancing over she just winks. She is right, I do need to let it go but the audacity of him to actually say that out loud? He may have said what everyone was thinking but really? Everyone on board understands he simply demonstrated plain old bad-manners, as my Grandmother would have said. He is lucky because a few years ago, I would have responded with some very un-lady like comments.

Our ride down from the eighteenth floor was quick and lucky for the jerk in the back, no more stops. Leading the zombie pack, we exit. I walk to the side of the lobby trying to avoid the departing stampede. Beginning to survey those exiting behind us, I point out three men that seemed to have exited last to Lana.

"See those men walking out the door?"

Lana turns and watches the group. "Oh yeah. Nice. Very nice. I like the way they look walking away except for that short one. I know I don't visit the gym like I should but he definitely needs to go."

With a little chuckle escaping me, I say, "Lana, I can always count on your honesty that I know for sure." Watching them as they exit, I continue, "I just bet one of those men was the ass kisser that made that ignorant comment. Who in the world ever heard of apologizing for to many people being on an elevator?"

Nodding her head in agreement, she says, "You know Charli, I have to agree. Even I wanted to respond to the idiot. My main thought was who actually rides the public elevator if you have a private one?"

"Good point, Lana. Who does do that and why would they?" My scrutiny continues, as we follow them across the lobby. "What do you think? I continue, "Just look at the way the shorter one is walking. It seems as if he is doing his best to keep up. I have no doubt he is the idiot as you so accurately described him. You know, I bet he kisses ass on every occasion that arises."

Holding her hand up to stop my ranting, Lana finally speaks. "Good gracious, Charli! Do what that kid's song my niece sings so much says, let it go. You want to grab some lunch? I am starving."

I know what she is doing, handling me. She always knows just what to say. Lana keeps me, along with my mouth, under control. Back in college, everyone knew who kept me from jumping off the tightrope I was walking while juggling so many things.

"Good idea, let's find something to eat around here. Now that you mention it, I am a little hungry."

Setting off to find a place to eat nearby, I pause to watch a tinted window navy Mercedes pull away. "That is a gorgeous car," I mumble to myself. Lana is two or three steps ahead when she stops, turns around and waits for me. As I catch up, her inquisition begins, "Charli, are you alright? What in the world are you stopping for? Are you coming or not?"

"Yes to the first and last questions. Why would you think that something is wrong?"

"Because, when I turned around you were mumbling to yourself. Just incase you have never noticed most people, especially the sane ones, do not do that."

Attempting to ignore her, I fight my urge to say something that I would more than likely regret later. I explain, "Lana don't tell me you didn't notice that fabulous car pulling away?"

She gives me her nose scrunch which translates into no, I did not. "Charli, you are the only woman I know that stops and admires cars like most women gaze at designer shoes."

"Brothers, Lana, brothers. Blame them. I learned to appreciate a great car way before I did a great pair of pumps. Which, I have you know, I stop and admire those too," I say as I stick the tip of my tongue out at her.

Shaking her head and walking on, my old friend says over her shoulder, "I am so glad. I only have a sister."

My head is actually beginning to hurt, stress induced more than likely. I know what is coming. With this type of pain, I need to get both food as well as meds into my body. Come to think of it, I really haven't had anything to eat substantially since brunch yesterday. Ok, so if I tell her, I'll get the lecture.

Charli, you know you can't treat your body that way. You of all people should understand that a good healthy diet is what keeps us all going

Looking at me as if I have suddenly grown a second head, she finally says, "So, let's go to this charming little bistro I saw earlier a couple of blocks down."

Knowing better than to argue, I agree

Attempting to help me focus on something other than the elevator incident she continues, "I bet whoever was in that car you were drooling over is off to a meeting about their next big deal. Probably buying up the world, one small company at a time. So, let's envision our future and discuss over lunch how you think our presentation was received."

I no more than get an agreement out when, Lana hails a taxi. "You amaze me, getting a taxi so easily. You'd make any New Yorker proud."

Smiling that big full mouth smile she winks as me saying, "Thanks, I had a lot of practice the year I interned at Gloss, Haney and Maine in the Big Apple." With the happy face transforming into a very serious one, "You know Charli, if we don't get The BC account, we'll be fine."

That is so Lana. Joking and laughing one minute and all business the next. "I know but think how much better off we would be if we do get it. It is the biggest project we've bid for since opening Supreme Corporate Travel." Deep down, we both know that having The Blaine Company as a client could make or break Supreme Corporate Travel. With so much of the competition utilizing technology and the internet, we've put the spin on us as having the intimate personal touch.

Houston Donovan

This morning meeting at my Miami branch is dragging. Lifting a brow as Johnson, the southern Florida manager, is droning on about statistics I can quote in my sleep I look to the end of the table studying the assembled group. Most seem as bored as I am. Underlining the note for Nash to compile background information on the key personnel within this office, I am seriously considering major changes after sitting through four hours of this. The reports being presented for review are lack luster, definitely not the quality of work I expect from my leaders. Frowning I evaluate the entire morning; unfortunately it has not surpassed my low expectations. A one word summary for this morning, tedious. Generally my philosophy is if my people have taken time away from another projects to put a presentation together for me, I will sit through it. At this moment, I have had enough. Pushing back from the conference table, I glance at my watch, doing something very uncharacteristic for me, interrupting the presentation. I stand causing everyone in the room to look toward me.

"Johnson, I believe this is an excellent place to break for lunch." Looking around the table, I can't help but recognize some relief on the faces of other executives from this office as I continue to speak, "We will pick up at this point in two hours." Without allowing time for any conversation, I walk past the new furniture I was surprised to find when I entered the office earlier today. Before I head into the washroom, I stop at my desk busying myself with some details that could actually wait until later. Anyone that knows anything about me should be able to read into my expression how displeased I am with the direction of this meeting.

Nash joins me at the elevator where we begin discussing a video conference I have with the Rome office later today. Nodding his head toward my door Nash clears his throat, "Sir, Melinda, has scheduled a lunch meeting with Johnson. Apparently, he would like to pitch a new proposal that he has developed."

Looking at him, he understands my displeasure at the thought of this. I have absolutely no idea what train of thought caused me to say, "Alright, this one time I will allow him to present informally. However, I want it made clear that this is the first and last time this will happen."

Nash has the good sense to stand quietly by as we are joined by Johnson. Before I have an opportunity to speak he asks, "Mr. Donovan, would you prefer to take the private one?" as we enter the elevator. "No this is fine." I step to the back. I actually would prefer it but somehow I get the feeling Johnson will start his pitch the moment we enter. The poor little man has no idea that I more than likely will never hear what he has to say. I somehow doubt that he will provide anything new or fresh if anything is based on this morning's presentation.

This is what I hate about public elevators, stopping on what seems like every floor as we descend from the thirtieth. At what point do people have enough sense to not step on when those already onboard are a tightly packed group? Somewhere around eighteen, the doors open revealing a simply stunning woman. The beauty is speaking to another woman whom I assume is her associate. They step into join us. As much as I am admiring her front I am equally happy when she turns around. Every male behind her is happy and appreciates that she joined us, as our eyes devour her ass in that tight skirt. Watching her, I notice how the light causes her shoulder length black hair to appear as if it has a blue cast to it. Damn, I'm getting hard as I adjust myself. It has been a day or two since I sunk myself into some moist heat.

Just about that time, Johnson begins prattling on about the private elevator, thinking to myself, can't he shut his mouth? I would have Nash toss Johnson off on the next stop but I prefer to keep my anonymity. This is my building. If I'd wanted to take the private elevator, doesn't the fool realize, I would have? These types of misunderstandings, actually more of a lack of understanding me, is what concerns me so about this office. For whatever reason, the overall personality, does not fall into character with my vision for this branch. The more Johnson speaks, the more convinced I become that I may need to look at relocation of several people, him being one. I really need to examine his profitability rates a little closer. This morning's meeting is not something I would list under the eagerness to repeat category. Generally, I look forward to visiting here, well until Johnson replaced Hannah Goldman. I am sorry we lost her. Thinking back to the day she alerted me that it would be the last time we were together, she was facing a wall, as I pounded into her eager pussy. Between gasps, I can still hear her say, "Houston, I am getting married."

My response might have been entirely selfish but I ask, "Why does that have to change anything? Doesn't he like to share?" I will miss the skills she brought to my boardroom but especially to my bedroom. I think about the wildcat she was. There were multiple times, the evidence remained on my back for several days.

Snapping back to reality, I must question Nash to find out what in the world he was thinking when he approached me about listening to this fool any longer than I must? Hell, what was I thinking when I agreed to it? I have a suspicion that Melinda, my new Miami assistant, might have had something to do with it. She has been glancing toward Nash quite a bit today. Obviously, she knows nothing about my friend Nash, or she would know it was a foregone conclusion that they will have an "experience." I believe that is what he calls his little fucking sessions. Shaking my head at the thought of how the military changed him. It still amazes me that he has such an open relationship with Cynthia. They both seem happy with their strange commitment of only being committed when Nash is in NYC. We exit the elevator, moving across the lobby as quickly as I can, Nash understands my pace. I doubt if Johnson has moved at this pace in years. Stepping onto the sidewalk, I see Jeff is leaning against the car waiting.

"Jeffery."

"Mr. Donovan."

Opening the back door, he picks up on our unspoken code. When I use his full name, as I rarely do, he knows my mood is generally not pleasant. I slide in across the seat allowing a space for Johnson. Sitting in the front with Jeff, Nash remains silent as my navy Mercedes pulls away from the curb. Both of my longtime friends sitting in the front, can interpret my temperament enough to understand I am unhappy at this moment. The fact that this will more than likely be the most excruciating meal I will endure during my month here causes me to frown at the thought. Simply hearing his voice makes me want to have Jeff stop the car just long enough to throw him to the curb.   That is twice I have thought about tossing him out of something within the last ten minutes. Johnson has no idea how lady luck is on his side at this very moment. I make a mental note to explore how he rose to the position of VP in Charge of the Miami Branch. Looking out the window, as we move along at a very slow pace by Miami standards I see a small restaurant up ahead. The quicker we get this started, the quicker this will be over.

"Jeffery, pullover. I want to eat at this little Bistro here on the corner." Meeting my eyes in the mirror, Jeff knows my moods enough that both he and Nash understand why I've just changed my plans.

"But Sir, I took the liberty of making reservations at my club. I had hoped to show you…"

I really don't think he wants me to respond to what he is saying so before the annoying little man beside me can get any further with his comment, I look across the seat at him as my lips tighten and my eyes narrow. He must have correctly interpreted my facial expression because he shut the hell up. Following with my request, Jeff pulls around allowing the four of us to quietly enter using the back entrance.

Chapter 3

Charli

After we order, I enjoy the charm of The Downtown Bistro. This must be one of the oldest buildings in Miami. I make a mental note to research it. Looking around, I can't believe my eyes and mutter to Lana to look who is sitting in the back of the room. In a small alcove, which ensures some privacy, sits the men from the elevator. Pointing this out to Lana, I also notice the person in the center, he is the essence of power. His wavy hair the color of milk chocolate makes me want to jump up, go over and run my hands through it. I really do have a thing for hair.

Lana lets out a little laugh.

"Oh goodness, did I say that out loud?"

"Yes, Charli you did say it out loud. You have always had a thing for men with good hair and saying things out loud that maybe you shouldn't. Even way back in college. Remember when you would say"… I hold up my hand to stop her.

"Ok, Lana I know, I know. I need to learn to control myself. Let's not go down memory lane."

Changing the subject I say, "It was a good presentation. Actually, great I thought."

Lana agrees and we decide to celebrate just a little tonight.

"So, Billy's it is then?" I ask, as I stand excusing myself to head to the restroom.

Just as I leave the ladies room, my phone vibrates. Stopping beside a small table in the hall, to read the text, my attention is drawn to some very old photographs depicting Miami during a different era. They are arranged around some period pieces that I find interesting. Looking around, I don't see a sign warning not to touch, I pick up a photograph to take a closer look because this stuff fascinates me. As I am examining it, someone bumps me from behind causing the frame to fall from my hands. I jerk my head around, only to come face to face with one of the men from the elevator. Providing one of the weakest apologies I believe in the history of the world, he sounds as if it was my fault he bumped into me. Finding more self control than I ever thought possible when I recognize his voice, I manage to mutter, "it's okay." If I say anything other than that, someone might mistake my annoyance for anger. Shaking my head just a little as he walks off, deciding to definitely tell Lana that we were correct the entire time. Our assumption of which person was so rude in the elevator was on target. It was the short man that was so annoyingly rude. I will have to share how I experienced his "charm" first hand.

Drawing on skills I mastered in my youth, when I found it advantageous not to respond to my brothers prodding and prying, silently I am counting one: stay quiet, taking a deep breath, two: don't do it, another deep breath, three: any type of response is simply not worth it. I bend down to pick up the photo. The jerk didn't even offer to pick it up for me. Real gentleman, for sure.) Successfully, talking myself out of saying something very un-lady like, I remain quiet.

I hear a deep masculine voice ask, "Is everything alright?"

Standing up, my eyes follow the voice. Low and behold standing beside me is the sex god with milk chocolate hair. Barely mumbling out a response, "Yes, everything is fine. No thanks to the jerk that just walked off."

Perfect Hair flashes me a smile that might possibly mess with my sanity. It is taking every ounce of my willpower to not reach up and touch his hair when he extends his hand to mine saying, "Here let me take this." As we briefly touch, a jolt of something runs through me. I jerk back quickly. He smiles again, as I attempt to laugh off that shock as best as I can.

"Thanks," is all I can utter.

As I turn to make my way back to our table, I realize that I must navigate a passageway which seems to have collapsed to a size barely large enough for me to move in. I now understand what it would feel like if you're the camel someone is trying to thread through the eye of a needle.

Making it back to the table, Lana looks up at me frowning. "I thought you got lost. What in the world happened?"

Sitting down, I smile feebly.

Lana being   Lana continues being the inquisitor, "Charli, are you alright?"

"Yes, why?"

Explaining my facial appearance she says, "Because you have a gleam in your eye that I haven't seen in years. Your face is flushed. What in the world?" Looking   toward   the   restroom   her interrogation continues, "Are you positive everything is fine?

Suddenly feeling a great need to escape the room I found interesting only a few minutes ago, I respond rather briskly, "I am positive I'm fine. Can we just get out of here?"

Nodding she stands, leading us out. As the door opens, all I think about is the man in the hall. The electrifying effect he had on me.

On the sidewalk, Lana pauses briefly then says, "Hey, check your phone, Joan tried to call you."

"Really? I didn't hear it. I received a text earlier but didn't notice a call." Snapping my fingers in a simple motion, I remember, I put it on silent just before our presentation; which means I simply failed to turn the volume back up.

Wrinkling her forehead, as I begin the search into my bag for the phone, she asks, "You are not

34

going to resort to the dump and find method as you call it, are you?"

Giving her a hint of the evil eye, I respond, "No." I am still digging.

Standing beside me, my best friend in the world seems just a little upset with me. Why? I actually have no idea. I explain, "Look, you know, I never and let me stress that again, never do I put my phone in the little pocket that purse designers so cleverly include for people like you, miss neat and tidy."

Laying my hands on it, I can see where I do in fact have four missed calls. "Yep, I see that now. What did she want?"

Grimacing a little, she responds, "A Blaine Company representative called."

"Ooo, that quick? Doesn't sound good does it?"

"No Charli, it doesn't really but what do I know? They requested for you to return the call, not me." Walking almost a block down the street, we agree that a call this important shouldn't be made in the public.

Telling her, "You head on back without me. My head has hurt all morning. I'm going to take advantage of the work for yourself thing. I'm going home, return this call, then find a dark, quiet room. Namely my bedroom and lay down for a-while."

"Ok, if you need me let me know. Are you positive you're alright?"

"Yes, I am." Not sure that quiet time is really what I want after looking into those chocolate eyes and feeling that jolt throughout my body but that is what I am going to get.

Just as we are about to get into the taxi, I realize I left my work bag by the table. "Lana, what's gotten into me? I've left my yellow bag at our table. It had all of the items from the presentation in it. You go ahead. I am going to retrieve it then head home."

Returning to the restaurant, only to find the table has been cleared and set for the next customers. Quickly looking around, I don't see it anywhere. I ask our server about it. Her answer just sends me into a mini rant, when she tells me she knows nothing about it. "Great! Just great. That was an expensive bag. Well expensive for me, at least."

"You can leave your name and number in case it turns up, Mam." Realizing it isn't her fault that I left my bag, I smile and do just as she instructed. Thank goodness it didn't have my laptop in it.

Chapter 4

Houston

"Sir, is something wrong?" I must have frowned when I sat down causing him to ask me a trivial question that he knows I hate.

"No, Nash I'm fine even better now that Johnson is gone. Where did he disappear to?"

Nash and Jeffery look at each other and then sitting in silence for just a moment, finally Nash responds. "He received a call just after he sat back down. Something about being needed back at the office."

"That's interesting that someone at the office would call him away from a lunch with the company's owner. Someone back there has balls. Remind me to find that person and thank them." I couldn't help a grin from forming on my face, "How fortunate for us boys. How fortunate for us." Looking from one to the other with neither showing any type of emotion, I continue, "Thanks guys. You two know how to make my problems disappear, don't you?"

"That would be why you pay us the big bucks, Boss Man." Continuing Jeff asks, "I noticed a frown when you sat back down, was there a specific reason?"

"No Jeff, no reason." Pointing to the front of the room, something under that table caught my eye as I was returning. I was focused on it. No doubt, something someone left behind."

Nash quickly looks around. "Where? I'll check it." Eyeing the object, he stands moving forward cautiously. Watching him, I am amazed as to how quickly he draws on his military training. Returning, with what appears to be a woman's laptop bag, Jeff simply can't contain the harassment that I see brewing. I never know what will set these two off but I would lay odds on the fact that a former top military man with numerous medals carrying a yellow woman's bag beside him will no doubt do the trick. Nash sits the bag on the seat beside him just as Jeff begins, "Hey Nash, I know expert bomb technicians like you can work in any situation."

Smiling and nodding his head, Nash proudly punching out his chest, "Yes, I can, Jeff."

"Like I was trying to say before I was rudely interrupted, if that bag you sat down has a bomb in it and you brought it back to this table, I'm going to give you the beating of your life after it's diffused, little brother."

"Dumbass, do you think I would bring it back to this table if it had a bomb in it? Especially, if Houston and I are seated here. Now if it was just you, I might consider it."

Shaking my head at the two of them, I am always amazed at the bickering they do. I know ninety-nine percent of the crap they throw at each other is just that, crap. Looking from one to the other, raising my fork to point to each in turn I continue, "Sometimes, I don't mind this girl fighting you two do but today it's getting on my nerves. Just shut it up."

I catch Nash winking at Jeff just about the time Jeff says, "The big man has spoken. Those of us that don't sit in the back of the car and wear five thousand dollar suits have received the message loud and clear."

With a twinkle in my eye, I respond, "If you don't stop running your mouth, you may find yourself without a job, old man."

"Old man, I am not that much older than you, Houston. I'm thirty-eight so that makes you what? Thirty-four. Old man, my ass."

Just as we were finishing our meal, they start at each other again. Jeff points at the bag sitting beside Nash, "You know, that shade of yellow is your color. I especially like that patterned scarf you've tied onto it. That print is *fabulous.*"

Nash responds to that snide little comment with a scowl. "Funny Jeff, very funny. If I didn't know you had a wife that loves to drag you to fashion week when we are in New York, I might be just a little concerned as to why you used the term *fabulous*, with that particular tone of voice. Even more concerning might be the fact that you commented on the patterned scarf."

Nash looks down at it lifting the ends rubbing them between his fingers, he continues, "Besides, it is a silk scarf by Jose Hernando if I was to guess."

"Really? You are giving me hell and you know the damn designer. Which brother should be worried about which?" Jeff asks.

"FYI, Bro" Nash responds with a sarcastic voice, using his breadstick as a pointer," I tend to know which designers utilize strong but sensual feeling products. You might be surprised to know that a great many ladies these days really enjoy their hands being restrained in some manner. If you were to up your game some, it might make my sister-in-law a happier woman."

I am beginning to question this conversation when I interrupt with, "Ok boys. Enough. If I didn't know any better, it sounds like this is the beginning of a cat-fight. It really does concern me though. I must confess, you two know way too much about women's clothing." Looking directly at Jeff, I continue, "By the way Jeff, as much as it pains me to admit this, Nash is correct about the bondage thing. You might try it just to have a different experience."

Jeff returns Houston's glare with only a grunt then says, " I'll be sure to provide a report if I decide to try it?" Looking at the two of us, Jeff breaks into a smile, as he continues, "I wish the hell both of you could see your faces. I suppose the thought of reading about my sexual prowess scares the two of you."

Giving a wicked little grin, Nash comments, "No, I do not need any type of report. The smile on my sister-in-laws face will be enough. By the way, it helps to know the terminology and designers these days if you are a single man. Especially if you don't have an untold number of zeros in your bank account."

Raising my hand, I suggest "You two need to get into the gym and pound out some of that brotherly love or sexual frustration from the way it sounds. Better yet, Jeff book us all three some time for the ring. I'll take the last man standing." Just as their bickering ends, I glance up to see that raven haired beauty re-enter. I'm unable to pull my eyes from her as she crosses the room to the table where Nash retrieved the bag. She looks underneath, turns and speaks with a server. Finally, she ends up at the counter. Nash must have seen her also, he begins to stand but I shake my head, no. Shrugging he sits back down, keeping the bag out of sight.

Who, in their right mind, is careless or forgetful enough to leave their bag behind? Typical airheaded female, I have no doubt, but she didn't sound like one during that brief exchange of words earlier. With the designer clothing she is dressed in, (who says I don't know women's designers?) I have no doubt that her focus when she was leaving was on

41

something other than her bag. This type of error in both personal and business life can be very serious, possibly deadly, especially with some of the people I deal with. Just a prime example of what I see on a daily basis, carelessness. No wonder most people don't succeed in business.

Charli

My head hurts! What in the world is that sound and where is it coming from? Whatever it is, it's very annoying. With each sound it feels like an ice pick stabbing away at my head. There it is again but it is a little louder. I think it is a beep I just am not sure. It doesn't really matter where the sound is coming from, I just want it to stop.

"Mom, what are you doing here?"

Why doesn't she answer me? My eyes are heavy as I struggle to open them just as I realize my phone is going off. Looking at it I see I have seven messages, most of them reminding me to be at Billy's tonight. The last one says,

Charli, I need u 2 b at Billy's tonight. Am making my mov. Need your support!!!!!!!!

I respond with a smile.

You have this. c… u … n … a… few.

Looking at my other text, I see Joan has also let me know someone dropped my bag off at the office. Thank goodness.

Lying on my bed a few minutes longer, I'm pondering if I really want to go tonight. My headache is gone. Maybe, a night out is what I need. Week nights at Billy's calls for nothing special-jeans, shirt and heels, which is a really good after the full on business attire from today. Even though I enjoy wearing a pencil skirt, silk blouse and pumps, casual sounds really good at this very minute. I drag myself off of the bed and to my closet.

Entering the bar, I hear the weeknight band playing something upbeat but not over the top. The floor to ceiling windows provide a breathtaking view of the city. It's nice that Billy's really isn't that far from my apartment. The bar staff makes great drinks, not weak like some places. A quick cab ride gets me home and in bed before my buzz disappears. A cab means no designated driver required. Several people are here with most gathered into groups in those soft leather chairs simply enjoying each other's company. A few are on the dance floor but everyone knows, Billy's dancing doesn't really start until after midnight which gives us the opportunity to chat without yelling.

Spotting Lana sitting across from Terrance, Rose, and some others I have met a few times I move to the group. We talk, we laugh and after a couple of lychee martinis I excuse myself and head to the restroom.

Glancing down at a table and behold sitting alone, twirling a tumbler of some gold liquid, is the man from lunch. He seems lost in thought almost brooding. I do know for sure that I would like to make him smile, which makes me smile. Glancing up just about the time I smile, our eyes meet for just a moment. Whew, the temperature of the room rose at least ten degrees. I wonder if he recognized me?

Ready to leave the restroom, I do a quick mirror check, deciding I'll speak to him. In the words of my brothers, what the hell. It must be fate that I see him three times in one day in a city the size of Miami. Yes, my hair looks good. Just a little fluff wouldn't hurt as I bend over. Raising back up, I check my teeth-nothing on them. I reapply my lipstick. Ok ready. I give myself a little pep talk- I can do this, I can do this.

With a deep breath I walk out ready to take one giant step, moving me forward into a new experience. As I near his table, I am ready. Unfortunately, he is no longer alone. Darn! So much for me sitting down and saying hello. Mr. Perfect Hair glances up from the stunning red head that is sitting across from him and our eyes meet, again, for just a moment. His thoughtful expression is now a scowl. I put an extra swing in my step and mumble the word smile.

Houston

I found this place purely by accident when I was driving through the city a couple of years ago. I have no doubt it can and does I am sure get loud as the night goes on. I have never remained here for that long. I do find Billy's a place where I can go without being hounded. No one here gives a damn as to who I am or what I own. I must admit it makes for a calm enjoyable evening.

"I think this place is boring. What do you think, handsome? Do you mind if I join you?"

Looking up, I raise my eyebrows. "Since you've taken the liberty of sitting down, why not? As to answer your first question about this establishment, obviously, I don't think it is boring. I wouldn't be sitting here if I did."

Seeing the beauty from lunch approaching, I can't help but think this night might be turning around especially if the woman sitting across from me will move on. Watching her move toward me, my eyes devour her well proportioned body. The jeans hug her hips perfectly, not to mention how well they fit through her thighs. I almost choke on my drink when I hear a gentle word escape from her luscious lips. Smile. I do as she walks on. Attempting to ignore the woman across from me and her mindless chatter, I signal the server.

Charli

Returning to our group, I decide to have one more drink and then head home. Terrance and Lana are on the dance floor as well as Rose and Joel, at least I think that is his name. T and Lana together, finally. I can only imagine I will hear all about it at the office tomorrow.

Glancing across the room, I notice the red head is still there. I was just about to turn to our server for another drink, when she sits one down in front of me. Picking my drink up, I realize the word smile is written on the base of the glass. I automatically look to the area of the room where my drink benefactor is sitting but unfortunately he seems engrossed in conversation with the woman. I shrug my shoulders just a little, smile and take a drink.

After a few minutes of conversation with those sitting around, I stand take my "smiling" cocktail over to the windows to enjoy the beautiful view of this city. It still fascinates me that my life has brought me to this place. Who would have thought? I am becoming just a little melancholy as I lose myself in the view. My mind is drifting back to a happier time when I understood the direction my life was moving. The course in which I am going is a little fuzzy at this point. Who am I kidding, the direction my life is taking is a lot fuzzy.

"Such a beautiful face looking at a striking view shouldn't look so sad."

Hearing this corny line causes me to glance over at the person standing beside me. I really must have been lost in the view, I had absolutely no idea anyone was this close. Of course, the drinks are not helping me maintain a vigilant alertness. Giving a small smile, I say nothing. I must admit, he is attractive in a nerdish kind of way.

Continuing to stand beside me for a few minutes longer, he finally introduces himself, "Huntington James."

"Hello, Mr. James, I agree the view out of these windows is beautiful. I wasn't sad, or rather I am not sad. I was simply losing myself in thoughts of days gone by. Actually those thoughts could sadden me if I allow them to."

"Well, let's push away those thoughts and lose ourselves in the music by dancing."

Pondering the statement, I reply, "sure why not." We head to the dance floor, just as the band goes into their retro set of songs which really is better for me because some of the current music is not my taste. Who am I kidding almost all of today's sound doesn't fit my taste. We dance through several upbeat songs, seems if right on cue when I need a break, a much slower number is beginning. I turn to head off the floor.

"Where are you going beautiful?"

"I need a drink, I am thirsty." As he directs me to a smaller more intimate table away from my group, I glance over and catch Lana's eyes. She gives me a questioning look as I slightly shake my head back at her.

We each order a drink. I decide to have another lychee martini. Huntington comments that he rarely if ever met a woman that ordered one of those. I shrug my shoulders explaining that the fruit is very sweet tasting but has a tropical taste at the same time. It doesn't take long for me to realize that Huntington James isn't interesting. He seems nice but as we sit I also notice the lighter skin on the ring finger of his left hand. Finishing my drink, I try as politely as possible to tell him that I am calling it a night. He really doesn't want to accept my refusal of another drink.

Looking him squarely in the eye, I begin, "Huntington, it would be my suggestion that you remember to do one of two things. Either, wear a ring on your left hand or take your wedding band off the minute you get out in the sun." The smile that was once on his face has disappeared as I continue. "My best advice is to think about why you married in the first place and keep it in your pants. Somewhere, I assume there is someone that loves you and would be deeply wounded by your actions tonight." His mouth drops open as I stand and walk away.

Returning to my original group, I sit with my back to the dance floor for a bit giving Huntington time to move on. Finally, I announce that I am going to head home. To a round of boos, I stand, do a quick check in Perfect Hair's direction but to my great disappointment he isn't there. I go over to pay my tab but find someone has beaten me to it. Attempting to quiz the bartender as to who paid it but he just smiles, hands me a card with a smiley face and a phone number written on it. You have got to be joking? This on top of the Huntington episode has thoroughly ticked me off. I am fed up with my night. Mumbling to myself, I acknowledge I have received the signal loud and clear, party gods. I'm going home for sure. I scan the bar once more not finding the face I am searching for. Thanking the bartender I turn to leave, stopping by the group telling them all goodnight. The more I think about that number the angrier I get. I take the elevator down to street level and hail a taxi the way I have watched Lana do it. OK, I might not have her skills but one stops. The minute I sit down, I jerk out my phone and send a text.

Thx 4 paying tab BUT NO THX!!! WHO DO U THINK U R?

Pushing send I say "take that!"

The taxi driver looks back at me in the mirror as if I am crazy. I am not sure if he is a smart man or just someone that doesn't want to hear another story by some lunatic. Whatever the cause, he simply drives on.

Arriving back at my apartment building, I storm into the lobby, only to find our kind night security guard. "Evening, Ms. Jensen. Is everything alright?"

"I'm fine, George thanks for asking. Just a little ticked off."

"Excuse me for saying so but I can tell. Sure hope I haven't done anything to upset you."

Looking at this man who has been nothing but helpful to me, I shouldn't take out my mood on him. "No, just a message I received earlier."

I feel my phone vibrate as I step into the elevator. Poor George probably thinks I have flipped my lid. I am still mumbling about him leaving a phone number for me as the elevator shoots me up to my floor. One of my bad habits is not being able to let things go, as my closest friends and family members know. I am still fuming as I unlock my door. My phone vibrates yet again to remind me, I have an unread text. I know who that message is from and I just can't wait to answer it.

You are most welcome. Houston Donovan

REALLY? Just like that? He thinks I was actually thanking him. Men!

Well, Houston Donovan u have some nerve!!!

There you go!!! I wonder if he can reign in his ego long enough to get the message?

Meaning?

Meaning! Dear Lord, this man must think really highly of himself.

Meaning leaving your phone number as if I want to possibly do more than say thank you for paying my tab. I don't know who you usually pay bar tabs for and what you get in return for that but you have the wrong person if you think I am ... Oh, Oh, Oh YOU ARE JUST TOO MUCH!!!

Almost immediately, my phone goes off announcing a test. *Shouting not necessary. A simple thank you would have worked.*

Thank you! Thank you! You have got to be kidding? I turn my phone off, put it on the charger and say to an empty room, "take that Mr. Houston Donovan."

As I step into the shower, my thoughts remain on a chocolate haired man with the name of the largest city in Texas. I remember how far away he appeared to be when I passed him the first time. I have no doubt a man that travels in his world has many things on his mind but good gracious does he have to be arrogant? I can't get it out of my mind how almost agitated he looked when I mumbled the word smile to him. Standing here in this long hot shower allowing the water to rush over my body has helped to calm me. My dreams are filled with dark haired smiling men, and shouting texts.

Chapter 5

Houston

Damn woman. Shouting at me through a text. However, after that little exchange, I sure won't mind hearing her shout when she is under me. I have absolutely no doubt that is where I will have her. She seems to be a spitfire. That is just what I need in my life, a little fire. I push away from my desk and lean back in my chair. Standing, I walk into and across the living space, sliding back a panel in what looks like a wall of glass. I remember now why I put off coming down here, damn heat. I close it. I'm edgy tonight.

Picking up my phone, I text one word. *Nash*

In response to my text, Nash walks into the room just as I rack the balls for a game of pool. Reading my mind, he selects his stick. It's game on. We play our usual two out of three with Nash winning easily tonight.

"What's wrong Hugh?"

"Restless, I suppose.

"Really? Nothing personal man but the Houston Donovan I know wouldn't have come home alone tonight which I'm assuming you did since we have shot two games of pool."

"Come home alone? Me? No, I didn't but she's gone. I sent her home not long after we got here. She was a redhead, a fake one at that, not my thing."

My remark stops Nash in his tracks. He looks at me with his left eyebrow raised, head cocked just a little to the right in what I've learned to interpret as his what the hell look. Without commenting, he continues to the fridge, grabs two beers, opening both on his way back to the table.

"Nice to know you feel at home here," I say as he leans against the table.

"Hugh, give it up man! We've known each other for what twelve, thirteen years?"

"About that."

"I can count on one hand the number of times I've seen you send a woman away."

Taking a long drink from my bottle, I finally break the silence, "I've got a number I want verified. It's on my desk."

"Tonight or in the morning?"

"Morning's fine but by eight"

"No problem"

"Oh and Nash, I need you to do it." We stand here leaning against the table just looking out into the night. Breaking our silence, I ask, "By the way, what was in that yellow bag?"

Shaking his head, "Not much. Typical woman stuff, along with what looks like a hard copy of a pretty good presentation for The Blaine Company.

Walking over to the window, I continue to stare into the vast nothingness across the Atlantic.

The Blaine Company. Hum. I might need to do something about that.

Charli

Joan enters my office with some items for me along with a small package. Looking up, as I say "Thanks Joan. Just sit it down, I'll get to it in a minute."

"Ok, by the looks of your desk, I think I'll just sit this stuff in this chair." Jokingly she adds, "If you ever want to see it."

Smiling, I wave my hand, "out, out."

Looking at my desk, she is right, it is a mess but developing a project for the philanthropist, J. Elliott Miltman requires a no holds barred presentation. If this gathering is as successful as we hope then his executive retreat might be our next step. That would mean Supreme Corporate Travel would have an excellent advantage over other companies for later excursions. J. Elliot will receive proposals for his elaborate gathering of friends/company executives from across the globe beginning in early August. Each year's retreat is held at a different worldwide venue. Since, next year's gathering will be hosted at his estate on the Keys in late spring our concept centers on the wealth and decadence of the nineteen twenties. With a wrap of the weekend being a costume party based upon movies from the era when men were men as the saying goes. I feel really good about this proposal. I should, I've spent untold hours on it.

Deciding to take a break, I open the mail Joan dropped off in my chair. Picking up the package I examine it. No return address. I'll have to remember to ask her about the delivery. As I open the envelope, I discover the contents. Taking it out, I begin to tremble.

As I lay it back inside, I begin yelling. "You have got to be kidding! He has some nerve!"

Both Lana and Joan burst into my office. Lana looks at me and asks, "Is everything alright?"

Almost yelling, "No everything's not alright! Look inside."

I jerk up my phone as Lana cautiously approaches. Joan is taking all this in with a look of confusion. She has never heard either of us yell, much less at each other. My dear friend Lana, carefully reaches into it, I can tell she is almost afraid of what she will lift out. When she raises her hand, she laughs.

"OMG, it's just a very large chocolate bar."

I snarl at her, "Look in it again."

This time Joan comes over, picks up the package, and pulls out a small card with two things handwritten on it, a phone number along with a smiley face. "What in the world?" Turning it over, looking at the back and rubbing the texture of it. "Charli, do you know this number?"

I don't respond as I jerk up my cell phone, and type *U must be joking?* Then I hit send.

"Yes, I know that number."

Looking across my desk, I recognize Lana's crossed arms stance, she isn't going anywhere until I explain. With confused looks on their faces, they listen to how this whole thing started. I omitted that Houston and I have been exchanging texts two or three times a day since that night.

"Charli, that was two weeks ago when we were at Billy's."

As Lana comments, Joan chirps in with, "This isn't the first envelope she has received, right Charli? I am pretty sure she has gotten the same package every other day this week."

"Well, he might be interested but believe me I am not! Who leaves their phone number like he did unless they're wanting one thing and only one thing-sex? I'll tell you who, a man that is so egotistical that he thinks women will drop at his feet. Namely one Houston Donovan. Now, I don't have any idea what your desk looks like but you can see mine and that should tell you, I have work to do."

Both, Lana and Joan look at me as if I am crazy, they turn and walk out the door. I hear Joan say over her shoulder, "I wonder who that might be?" as my phone buzzes, with an emoticon of a smiling face. My response is a frowning face. I put my phone in my bag. I don't want to deal with him. I have work to do.

Needing a brief break, I walk out into our outer office just as a package arrives. I sign for it, look at the name and realize it's for me. The return address on this wrinkled envelope I am holding is causing me to hesitate opening it. I have a decent idea what will be in it though. I am being dishonest with myself. I have no idea what is in the package, but I am pretty sure it will be accompanied by a phone number and a stupid smiley face. Returning to my office, I sit down behind my cluttered desk and lean back in my chair. I turn the manila envelope in my hands examining it thoroughly. What am I doing? I don't back away from things. Using my letter opener to attack the packing tape it's sealed with, I finally reach the contents. With some trepidation, I reach in and pull out a small, lightweight book. No, it's not a book but more of a journal. Not a journal because it has a title. Listen to me rattling on. The title just sets me off.

Communication Techniques
A Manual for the Socially Weary Female

What in the world is this? I am absolutely going to kill him. If I could get my hands on him right now I would choke him. Yes, that is exactly what I would do. I would choke him till that smug smile was right off his face.

57

I am yelling as both Lana and Joan enter. Lana looks at me and asks, "Is everything alright?"

Throwing my hands in the air I respond, "I wish everyone would stop asking that. Do I sound alright? No everything's not alright! Look at this thing!" As I stick the journal/book out at them. Being brave, Joan reaches out and removes the reprehensible thing from me.

Examining it, she says, "This is beautiful. Charli, look at this leather cover."

"You may think it is beautiful Joan but I think it is horrible. From a man that is just as irritating. Get that thing out of my sight!"

As straight faced as she can possibly be, Joan hands "the thing" to Lana. She looks at it, turns it over and examined the back of it. If Lana knows what is good for her, she won't do what that mischievous grin is preparing me for. She opens her mouth and not a word comes out. What does escape from her is a howl of laughter that brakes my barrier down.

The next thing I know we are all laughing so hard that if someone had entered the outer office they would have mistaken us for escapees from the happy farm. Wiping the tears away from our faces, I look at them and suggest we all get back to work. My cell rings. I ignore it. It rings again. I ignore it again. My phone rings, guess what I do? I ignore it. I don't want to be disturbed so it goes to voice mail. I mute the darn thing and dive back into work. I am putting together the presentation for the Miltman Affair weekend and need to remain focused.

As I stuff my laptop into my bag, I look over my desk to make sure I have everything. I look at the book. Jerking it up, I mumble. "Might as well take this." I stuff it into my bag, shaking my head in wonderment as to why I am bothering to take it home with me. Knowing those two busy bodies that skulk around the office, I will never hear the end of it. Hopefully, out of sight-out of mind. Who am I kidding? I love those two even if they really do irritate me beyond no end. I also know, there is absolutely no way they will allow me to forget this. I can see my dear friend, Lana, reminding me about this object until the day we die. Lord.

Chapter 6

Escaping the workday out the back door, I walk over to my good old Ford. Well, it's actually only a couple of years old. Somehow, it just sounds right to say that. I suppose that is the Midwest girl that I thought was buried deep down within breaking out. Just about the time I open my car door, the back door to our building closes.

"Hey."

Squeezing my eyes tight I'm willing myself to remain calm. Maybe, I should count to ten before I answer. Who am I kidding, that won't help.

"Wait a sec. I have a quick question."

Putting my yellow bag in the back seat, I stand there for just about a minute, before I turn around. "What is it Lana?"

"Did you get your reading material for tonight?"

Attempting, to sound confused, I answer, "What? What reading material? I'm not taking any work home with me, tonight. My plans are actually vegging out in front of the TV."

"You know, your new reading material to help with your communication techniques," she laughingly replies.

Sharing my death ray glare with my dear friend, I say, "I tell you what, Missy, when I finish it, how about I loan it to you? We can compare our notes on what revelations we garnered from it."

Smiling that famous Lana smile, she replies, "Ha! Ha! Very funny. I've never had a man complain about my communication skills."

As if it just hit her I am standing beside my car, she says, "Hey, I didn't know you drove today. What's up with that?"

She's managing me again. Nodding my head and patting the roof, "Yep, as you can see I sure did. I just felt like it this morning but now I wish common sense had taken over and prevented me from doing something stupid like driving." Sounding like some kind of broken record, huffing just a little, I explain, "That's about the only thing I dislike here. I know it is only five blocks to my place but I bet I will have to defend my life at least once on each block. People are crazy drivers."

Putting one hand on her hip, Lana just stands there without saying much. "I don't drive here so I have no comment. Hey, by the way, feeble attempt at changing the subject."

"I knew it. I just knew you wouldn't leave it alone."

She continues, "Seriously, he must be attracted, Charli. I doubt he would still be contacting you if he isn't. I think this is a good thing for you. I know you don't research men but just give me the word and it's done." Walking over to join me at the car Lana has a smile on that innocent looking face. I sit down then answer, "Yeah, I know. Did you see him, Lana? He is gorgeous."

"Honey, that doesn't describe him. He is H-O-T. Heck, I'm attracted to him. Who wouldn't be? Maybe, a blind woman?"

Shaking my head, I finally reveal my actual thoughts. "I don't know, Lana. Something just doesn't feel right. Men that look like him don't go for women that look like me. He must have some type of serious defect. It must be internal because I didn't see anything on the outside that even hinted at a defect."

"Seriously? I can't believe I am hearing this from you. You haven't always felt that way about yourself Charli. Besides have you looked in the mirror lately? Girl, you are not too shabby yourself."

Suddenly, I feel as if the weight of the world has just dropped onto my shoulders. "Thanks but the scars are still here. Who am I kidding? They will always be here both the physical ones as well as the mental ones." I say as I gently tap my head against the steering wheel. My real emotions must be showing on my face as I look back up at her. Thank goodness, I have sunglasses on.

Lana calmly asks, "Have you talked to him, at all?"

"No. Don't intend to," as I wipe a tear from my eye.

"Well, alright then. If that is the way you feel, enough has been said." Lana possesses some sixth sense and seems to know just when I need a hug. Holding her arms out, "Come here you. I hope you know, you deserve happiness."

Standing in our parking lot, hugging my best friend feels the most natural thing in the world. Lord knows, her hugs have gotten me through plenty. I will never be able to repay her for all the things she has done for me.

"Thanks." I turn around get back into my car. "See you tomorrow," I say as I close the door.

As I enter my apartment, I toss my keys in the bowl beside the door, set my bag down and move into the living room. Sitting down on the sofa, I lay my head back and reflect on the day. I really have no idea how I feel about Houston. I must admit I have enjoyed the banter we have exchanged these past few weeks. I don't know why he gets under my skin so much. Looking over at my bag, I can't decide what to do. Whether to get the thing out, look at it or just toss it. Deciding to look at it, I move cautiously. Reaching into my bag, I pull it out. It is a beautiful book. The soft worn leather as well as the gold embossing feels almost sensual as I run my hands across the cover.

Taking the book with me, I lay it down on my dining room table as I prepare a grilled chicken salad. Returning to the thing, I pick it up and begin to thumb through the contents. I really can't imagine having to follow some of the ridiculous things I am reading. Just as I finish my meal, I can't help but smile. I know exactly what I am going to do just as soon as I load the dishwasher. I go in search of my phone. With a bit of a laugh I develop my response to Houston's gift.

Houston

Tossing the papers onto my desk, I glance at my watch. I expected some type of response from Ms. Jensen about my little gift that I had delivered to her earlier today. Nash and I are elbow deep in some sensitive issues that must be taken care of. The aviation branch of Highland Diversified seems to be facing a very difficult lawsuit. Our attorneys have been battling this for years but it seems as if we will actually be going to trial. Shaking my head, I simply am having a difficult time focusing. When Nash calls me on it, my only response is "I have absolutely no idea why I am spending so much time focused on Charli Jensen, Nash. It seems as if I can't get her out of my mind."

Sitting across from my desk, he responds, "Damn Hugh, I know why. She is the first woman in as long as I have known you that has made you work for it. She isn't falling for that Donovan smile."

Leaning back in my chair, I take a moment to process what he has just said. "You know, that is more than likely it. She is difficult as well as stubborn. I should be giving all of my attention to this pending legal action and I can only think about the action I want to give to her."

"You have got it bad. I never thought I would see the day, that Houston Donovan would have difficulty getting the woman of his choice in bed."

Just about the time we are pouring over some old medical reports, my phone goes off. Picking it up, I read the text.

A hint from your gift:
Rather be silent than talk nonsense

Laying my phone down, Nash gives me a questioning look. Ignoring him and the text, I return to the report we are discussing. Later when we take a break, I decide to respond.

What I want doesn't require talking.
Moaning, yes. Talking no.

Charli

I stop by Lana's office the next morning catching Joan in there as well. "Good morning, ladies. How's the world treating you this fine morning? I saw that! You two looking like I've lost my marbles. Can't a woman be in a really, really good mood in the morning?"

At almost the same time, I heard them both say, "No." Then Joan follows up with, "Well not you anyway." Lana must have realized how that sounded because she jumped in with, "Charli Jensen, I have known you for almost fifteen years and you have never in all that time been a morning person, not one time. What's up?"

Raising my right hand, "I swear nothing is up. I just slept really, really well last night, that's all. I am very rested. At this moment, I feel as if I could take on the world. Hey, what about a drink after work today? Besides, I really owe the two of you an apology for all my bitchiness lately."

"I don't know why you think you owe us any apologies, Charli, that's just who you are," Lana said smiling.

Scrunching my forehead as if I am confused and placing my hand on my chest, "Who says I should be the only one apologizing, Lana?"

"All three of us have been working really hard lately," Lana replied, "but it is also beginning to pay off. I think we could all use a couple of drinks, just to relax."

"I'm up for a drink tonight minus the shop talk. What about you Lana? Joan?"

"OK, Charli, you're right about needing some "girl talk" time. We all three need to remember to enjoy this time in our lives," Joan replies smiling.

Our business reputation is growing right along with our funds. Granted landing The Blaine Company's account, would have helped us really get our name out there more but we haven't done bad. I suppose I am being impatient. It's just I want the success. No, I need the success. So many things have gone wrong in my life, I just need something good for once.

"Ok ladies, let's get out of here and get our girl groove on, I say as I walk out to the front, where Joan is tap, tap, tapping away on her keyboard. She looks up, "Give me about ten minutes."

I poke my head into Lana's office, I mouth ten minutes when I realize she is on her cell. My phone is dancing the cha-cha across my desk as I enter my office.

"Aren't you going to answer that?" I shake my head at Lana as she walks into the room.

She smiles, then says "Let's see, the first round must be work related because we just booked Atwood Aviation. That is who I was on the phone with just now." Swallowing hard, I just look at her. Lana knows how I feel about planes.

Closing my laptop, "Let's lock up and get out of here." Meeting in the lobby, we stood discussing the pros/cons of the places around us, we decide Chester's. It's one of those national chains that has a restaurant/ bar combo. After a brief, actually very brief discussion, we agree to walk the three blocks. We each head back to our desks to change shoes. Walking might justify some nachos/cheese that Chester's is known for.

"Let's go ladies, my stomach is rumbling." Since we can't all walk side by side, I step back letting Joan and Lana out first. I lock up, turn around and stop dead in my tracks.

There he is. Mr. Darn Good Looking Donovan in all his glory propped against a navy SUV that probably costs more than what I made last year. His arrogance radiates from him. No arrogance isn't the word, it's more like haughty. Eureka! That's it. Haughtiness. Never in a million years, would I admit this to him but damn any man that looks like him has good reason to be arrogant along with haughty. It's his stance: hands tucked into his pockets, jacket unbuttoned, tie loosened and his feet crossed. Topping it off are those piercing eyes peering at me over his black aviator sunglasses. There is only one word to describe him, HOT.

Slightly nodding his head, he simply says, "Ms. Jensen, Ladies." The way he just said my name drips sex. I could throw him down, and devour him right here in the middle of this street. I am not sure it would be good for my reputation let alone Supreme Corporate Travel's reputation for the headlines to feature me attacking a man on the street for sex.

"Mr. Donovan," I say without showing any emotion. The girls are looking back and forth between the two of us. I will absolutely kill them if either one of them says a word or makes a sound.

"May I have a word?"

I shake my head slightly, turn away and begin walking. I try to gracefully stomp (Can you stomp gracefully?) past the girls leaving them behind hustling to catch up. I can't believe him.

Lana asks, "Ah, Charli what would a "word" hurt?"

If looks could kill, I think my best friend would at least be falling to the ground with a death pallor consuming her at this very moment. "Lana who the hell says that? Just tell me."

Lana stops, looks back, looks at me and mumbles with just a hint of a smile, "Ah, apparently Mr. Donovan?"

"You aren't going to shut up are you?" is just about all I can manage to say. I don't know who to be the most upset with, her or Joan. Both of them seem to think I am insane for not having a word as he said.

Looking at me, Joan points to Lana and pipes in with "If she shuts up, I'll start in."

I close my eyes, take a deep breath and turn around. Lord, he is delicious. Retracing my steps back to him, I stop directly in front of him where he gives me that smile. If I didn't know any better, I would swear my panties just melted away.

"Yes, Mr. Donovan?"

"Houston."

"Mr. Donovan, is that the word you wanted to have with me? Let me see if I understand this, all the time we have been texting, all you really wanted to discuss is how I should address you? Ok, we've established that so I'll be off."

As I am turning away, he gently touches my arm. This time it isn't just my arm tingling. My entire body is heating up from that simple action. Stopping me, he says, "I really don't think so."

I'm trying my very best to be really ticked off, after that comment, but I can't. Crap, any other time a man would have dared to say that to me, all he would be seeing was my back as I walk away. My heart is racing, as if I have just completed a marathon. Standing here, I follow his gaze as he looks down the sidewalk beyond Lana and Joan. I can't help but wonder what has caught his eye. More than likely, another woman if he is anything like the few men that I have met from his social circle.

Finally, he asks, "Where were the three of you off to?"

"Chester's Bar and Grill. Why?"

Leaving me standing, he walks the ten or so steps over to the girls, has a brief word and the three of them return.

Looking me in the eye, Houston says, "We'll give the three of you a lift to Chester's."

Giving them my wrinkled nose face, all three of them could interpret its meaning. Sheepishly, Lana explains, "I didn't want to tell you but my feet are hurting. The thoughts of walking three blocks is making them hurt even more. Mr. Donovan has offered us a ride. I agreed."

Looking over at Joan, she chips in with, "I agreed also, Charli."

Taking a very deep breath, I must admit I would feel silly walking by myself so I give in. Before Joan can open the front door, the driver comes around getting it for her. I recognize him from the first day that I was unlucky enough for my path to cross with one Houston Donovan.

Not bothering to look at the driver, he continues, "Nash, we'll drop the ladies at the Chester's Bar and Grill just down the street."

Chapter 7

Arriving at Chester's in what seemed five minutes or less, (This man sure drove as if he was a native Miamian.) I suggest Lana and Joan go on in. Both of them seem a little unsure about getting out and leaving me behind. "It's ok, go on. I'll be inside in a few minutes."

As Lana is opening her door I reach over, touch her arm and say "Hey, wait about ten minutes, then order me a Sidecar instead of a Margarita."

Lana looks at me as if I had suddenly grown a second head, "Sure. I'll wait ten minutes and order you a Sidecar."

Looking out the window, I watch them as they are talking to Nash. Sometime during my thirty-two years, I've finally learned to trust my instincts. At this moment, they are telling me I am the topic of conversation out there in the middle of Chester's parking lot. My instincts are also telling me that I'm not going inside. The realization hits me, from the moment I agreed to the ride, my night with the girls had been eliminated.

Looking toward him with questioning eyes, "I'm not going inside am I?" I ask even though I really don't need an answer.

He turns in his seat giving me the full on frontal view allowing our eyes to meet. Those eyes! My Lord, why in the world didn't I notice them before? I mean, I did notice them but I have been so focused on his hair that they really didn't register. They are like pools of warm milk chocolate, not warm chocolate but rather hot chocolate with steam rising from them. I could definitely get lost in them. Snapping out of the daze I'm finding myself in, I slide over to occupy a space closer to the door.

In response to my question, he calmly states but with a hint of a patronizing tone, "Charli, I can assure you that is your decision not mine. I am not in the habit of kidnapping. I can firmly state for the record, any woman I am with is most definitely doing so of her own free will."

Almost stuttering, which is something I haven't done in many years, I hurl my response, "Well that's good to know." As if an invisible switch has been flipped, it is all I can do to contain myself. I am experiencing one of those movie moments. The minute in the movie when the woman realizes she is attracted to someone her instincts tells her she shouldn't be.

"You changed your choice of cocktail to a "Sidecar. I find that interesting. Since I heard you mention it I have been sitting here, trying to remember if anyone I know ever orders a Sidecar."

"Mr. Donovan, I…"

"Houston, must I continue to repeat myself?"

Taking a deep breath, I begin to explain. "Houston, I like unique things. I have always been

73

one of those woman that prefers antiques to modern. I have always been drawn to vintage items, so when I think of a Sidecar, I visualize old black and white movies. Crazy, I know."

Smiling a panty melting smile he responds, "Then you must have enjoyed my little antique gift to you yesterday."

Rolling my eyes as I turn to face him, I can only say, "Sure, I did. I thought it terribly amusing."

Ignoring my comment, he shakes his head and continues, "As for the Sidecar, I can assure you, it is not crazy. We all have our little quirks. Charli, one thing we have in common is liking unique things. I have spent just about every day of my adult life searching for unique things in one form or another. Now as far as the vintage, I disagree. I like new, modern things."

Thinking I might get the subject off me, I calmly ask, "Did you know the Sidecar was supposedly created in Paris?"

With somewhat of an amused little laugh Houston continues, "No, I didn't, sweet lady. You seem to have some knowledge of its origin so I am assuming you drink it often."

"No, I mean yes I do like it but I rarely drink it. I know about its existence because of research I recently conducted for a proposal we presented."

He turns away from me, and looks out the window for what seems like a long time but in reality was only a brief minute or two, I am sure.

It's not like I got out my stopwatch but I finally broke the silence by asking, "Houston, why did you come to my office? I know we have exchanged some snippy, as well as interesting texts but I really don't quite understand what we are doing?"

"Turning back to me his facial expression has changed; it is as if he has a revelation. When he speaks his tone takes on an almost solemn quality. "There is an event later this year that I originally planned to discuss with you. However, I have changed my mind."

"Oh ok. So why are you telling me this?"

"Patience Charli, patience. I have come to notice in our exchanges that is not one of your strongest areas."

Opening my mouth to spout a reply, I think better when he raises his eyebrows silently saying, just as I expected. Ha! Mr. Donovan. I fooled you.

Continuing on, "This event is quite the social affair in my circle, which translates into a great deal of organization being required."

Keeping my hands folded in my lap, I press my thumbs together to keep me focused and to not let my temper get the best of me. "Let me give you a little piece of information about what I do, I organize corporate events, recreational usually, so believe me I understand what it takes to bring together an event." It is if a ton of bricks has hit me on the head, I had that instinctive feeling again. "Wait a minute, are you asking me to do some type of work for this whatever?"

"Good Lord no. Those pieces are handled in advance, often years." Continuing on, "You would have the opportunity to create what could possibly be some valuable contacts to introduce Supreme Corporate Travel to." Running his hand through his hair, as if he is somewhat irritated, he exhales and continues. "This event is very exclusive with some extremely influential people attending. It is quite the gathering of individuals from various industries." In my social circles, The Black and Gold Gala is one of the premier events. The Gala attendees, as the name describes, are required to dress in either or both of the two colors. Visually, it is spectacular."

Smiling, I gently touch his arm. "I know you will find this very difficult to believe, I'm naturally not a rude person but is there a point to this conversation?"

He sits here as if he has the weight of the world on his shoulders at this very moment. He doesn't reply so I forge ahead in this conversation. "Is that what you wanted to talk to me about? Thanks for thinking of SCT. I appreciate it honestly but since I have never heard of this Black and Gold Gala I really can't be upset that you have changed your mind."

Confused somewhat by this strange conversation I continue, "Houston, I have a drink waiting for me inside."

Turning to face me, he smiles just a little sheepishly, then says, "No actually, you more than likely don't. I am sure Nash anticipated we would be awhile and that your drink would be getting warm. Which means he would have told your friends not to order for you."

Taking a deep breath, I can't decide who to be upset with, him or Nash. Maybe neither. Nash was anticipating my needs. From what Houston has just said, Nash understands his cocktails as does Houston, apparently. They both know my drink wouldn't come with ice and to truly enjoy a Sidecar, it must be consumed soon after it is created while the contents are cool. Houston calls Nash to inquire about my missing cocktail.

Houston's eyes meet mine, he nods and smiles. While he is wrapping up his call, I send Lana a text.

Somehow, think you already know. I think my plans just changed. Probably not coming in.   C... U... N morning.

Chapter 8

Houston raises his eyebrows just a little as I move to the seat near the door. "You might bite" I give him just a small smile.

"Only if you want me to, Ms. Jensen. Only if you want me to." He replies almost wickedly. I'm not sure if it is his physical response or the playful, at least I hope playful, comment that gives me a warm feeling. Who am I joking, it is a totally hot thought. I don't really know about a bite but a nibble in certain places would be just fine with me.

As we speed along, I notice we are going down I-95. I have absolutely no idea where we're heading but this is the first time in a very long time that I have been ok with not really knowing. I glance over and realize Houston is looking at me.

Trying to sound calmer than I am actually feeling, I ask, "What?"

Replying with something a little less than a snicker, because men like him don't snicker I am sure, he simply states, "I was wondering just how long it would take you to begin questioning our destination."

Darn, how can I ask without sounding strange? Looking over at this man that screams power, wealth and influence, I say, "Now that you mention it, I notice we are on 95."

He reveals, "We are headed to Coral Gables"

"Oh, ok. It's a relief to know that you're not rushing me off to be sold in a human trafficking plot that you hear about."

"No I am not. For the record, my beauty, I have already stated I don't kidnap women. Charli, while I am sure you are trying your best to be humorous, I can only hope that isn't a topic or thought that you find in the least bit possible."

Turning my head, it's all I can do not to let my mouth literally fall open. I do manage to get out, "No of course, I don't."

It takes me a minute to gather my wits after that. Finally, I feel ready to inquire, "What's in Coral Gables?" Without pausing, I give up a little about myself. "You know, I've lived in the Miami area for a little over a year and never been to Coral Gables."

Beginning to let his guard down somewhat, I can see a normal conversation transpiring between us, Houston continues, "Really? I try to get out there at least every other time I am in Miami."

Trying not to sound disappointed or prying I attempt to carry on, "Oh, you don't live here? In Miami, I mean."

Shaking his head as he speaks, "No, I have regional offices here that I visit frequently."

"For some reason, I assumed you lived here." Pausing for just a bit, that is when I realize I am enjoying this conversation. No banter. No one trying to one up the other. It is nice. Oh my, I hope he doesn't realize I am enjoying this so much.

"No, while I do like the warmth, the summer heat is just a little too much for me. I really prefer the four seasons."

Smiling, I give one of my little chuckles as I am immediately reminded of something I was told when I first moved here. "You know, I made a comment similar to that to a native Miamian once. He laughed at me and said we may not have four seasons but we do have two, hurricane and tourist. I didn't really understand at first but now I completely get it."

Bobbing his head up and down, he explains, "We are heading to The Museum and Gardens of Biscayne. I thought this might be an interesting place for us to share. You seemed to be focused on the old photograph at lunch that day."

I smile. I am not sure if it's because he remembers the first day we met or if the smile is due to the fact that I am sitting beside the best looking man I have ever laid my eyes on. While pondering the answer I notice Nash is driving through a gate. On the inside of this gated area is a drive leading to a villa with stunning greenery and foliage. As the three of us exit the SUV, I notice most people are leaving the grounds. A security guard approaches us but Nash steps in and has a conversation with him. I glance up at Houston who is continuing to walk as if the man doesn't exist. The guard nods his head, turns away and begins talking on a walkie talkie type radio. I wonder what that was all about but I don't mention it. Neither, Houston or Nash, make a comment. I suppose that kind of stuff happens to him regularly.

Walking silently through this stunning estate, I feel the grandeur of America's wealthy from years gone by. Strolling side by side with Houston through, what must be European inspired, grounds I feel oddly calm. It was obvious immediately as he guided us to a stunning courtyard that he was familiar with this phenomenal place. Standing at the entrance of what the plaque on the side of the archway identifies as The Secret Gardens, I am enthralled.

Speaking in a calm voice, that was missing from our earlier conversation, Houston breaks the silence. "The first time I came here, I was moved by the beauty and tranquility I felt." Looking around, he finally continues with a deep sigh, "I plan to get out here every time I am in Miami but as I stated earlier it is more like every other time I visit, which means a couple times a year. "

Smiling, as my eyes move throughout the scene lying in front of me, it seems as if they are drawn to the stones throughout the garden. They seem to create a freestanding wall. "I certainly can understand why" is my only comment as my eyes continue to take in the beauty.

Gently placing his hand on the small of my back, he guides me across a moss outlined pathway. I must admit, I like his hand there. It feels nice. Heck, who am I kidding, it feels fantastic. The heat from our brief touch earlier has quickly returned. Only this time, it is rapidly spreading throughout my body.

We stop at the opposite end of the entrance. Where two cocktail glasses sit on a top step near an enclosed alcove. I can feel a change in the air around us. It feels as if a storm is brewing on the horizon. Houston must feel it also. There is simply no way he can't.

Attempting to calm the tempest brewing between us he jokingly comments, "Mademoiselle, I believe you ordered a Sidecar earlier. I would never want to come between a lady and her beverage."

Tilting my head and responding in one of the few French words I am familiar with, "Why thank you monsieur." I am truly fascinated as to how he arranged this in the small amount of time since we left the parking lot.

Moving to the top of the steps, I am almost eye level with Houston as he hands my drink to me. Tilting my head a tiny bit, I find his smoldering eyes focused on my face. I wonder, if my eyes mirror the passion I see in his.

"Come here, Charli." Before I can respond, his hands are on my waist pulling me to him, only stopping when I am completely against him. This action causes me to drop the cocktail glass where it shatters as it hits the ground. "I am going to kiss you.

I've wanted this since I saw you standing beside that table lost in those photographs."

"Houston," a light sigh escapes from me as we melt together like ice cubes in the hot Florida sun. My hands find their way to his broad shoulders steadying myself. I have no idea how long we stayed locked in that kiss savoring the feel of each other. Warmth is spreading through my body at such a level of intensity, I'm not sure if I will be able to stand alone when his firm lips leave mine. Leaving my hands on his shoulders, to steady myself, I realize from the minute we separate, this isn't the only kiss we will share. I keep my eyes closed just for that extra second trying to savor the last moments of our connection. A connection that I already want again. Looking down, I step back to collect myself. Problem is, I am not sure I really want to.

As he speaks, Houston steps toward me. "Charli, I have many talents."

I begin stepping backward. Interrupting him, smiling provocatively, "Of that I have no doubt." I continue moving backward attempting to put enough space between us to allow me to think.

"One of my talents is reading people and anticipating their needs."

Stepping slowing backward, all I can manage to mutter is, "Oh." I reach my limit, literally, as I am backed up against a stone wall.

Continuing forward until there is maybe a couple of inches between us, he places his palms on each side of my head against the wall. Leaning into me, I feel his hot breath as he whispers in my ear, "For example, at this moment, I know you want me as much as I want you." Without waiting for any type of response from me, he bends to my neck, blowing his hot breath in a trail against me, ending with his mouth finding mine.

Breaking our kiss as I put my hands on his chest. (Oh my. He feels so good.) "I don't know what came over me, Houston. I certainly do not act like I just did with men I don't know."

Backing away from me, he asks in a tone I am unsure of, "Charli, what did we just do?

I stood there without answering him, he continues on. "We shared passionate kisses in a romantic setting. That is something any sane man would want to experience with a woman as beautiful as you."

A shocked expression must have come across my face at that comment because he continued, "You are, you know? Beautiful."

Smiling feebly, all I can say to his compliment is, "Thank you."

"We are both consenting adults. I can assure you, we have done nothing inappropriate. I must admit, I would like to change that. " Briefly looking down at the shattered glass, "Of course, someone on staff will believe that the broken shards of an antique cocktail glass is wrong. Perhaps, that is our cue to leave. How do you feel about leaving the scene of the crime?"

Laughing just a little, I agree that might be our best plan. Again, placing his hand on my back guiding me out of this magical place, we retrace our footsteps. Sneaking away, as if we are actually escaping a crime scene. From somewhere behind us, I hear some type of whirring noise. Pausing, we both turn around, to find his driver, Nash I think, pulling up beside us in a four seat golf cart.

Winking at me, Houston bows a deep bow saying, "Lovely lady, your chariot awaits."

Falling into the roll, I give a mock curtsy asking, "If this is my chariot are you my Knight in shining armor my dear sir?"

"I don't know about being a knight but if that is what you want me to be, then yes I will be your knight." Flashing me a sexy smile, he nods toward the front saying, "but I hope Nash doesn't turn into a rat at sundown."

Nash quickly replies, "I hope not either sir, I hope not either." We all laugh as Nash whips us through the grounds.

Chapter 9

As Nash expertly zips back up I-95, returning us into the city, Houston turns toward me, stretching out his seatbelt to place his left arm across the seat back. Giving me his oh so sexy grin, "If you are up for another attempt at having a Sidecar, I'd be happy to try my hand at creating one."

Lost in examining his dimple but not wanting this evening to end, I give the old pretend you're thinking expression, "They say third time's the charm, but I think I am giving up on the Sidecar tonight."

Looking somewhat surprised, he replies, "Oh, alright."

Raising my eyes up to meet his in what I hope is at least seductive, I quickly add, "Maybe I should focus on a nice glass of wine."

Smiling, he touches my shoulder as he gently brushes my hair back, he takes on a serious tone. Actually a very serious one as he asks, "Did you hear that?"

Looking around me, I shake my head, "No, I didn't hear a thing. What was it?"

"I believe that was my cognac moaning because the ingredients for your Sidecar will not be needed."

I swat at him, "Really?"

"Yes, really." Moving his hand up to cup my chin, he traces my lower lip ever so gently with his thumb. "Which in turn means, the cognac will not get to touch these luscious lips."

Smiling back at him, "So that was your cognac making that sound? Wow, that is some alcohol. It must taste very special. Come to think of it, I've never heard of any cognac that could make sounds."

"Of course it tastes special. I must admit, it isn't actually the cognac that makes the sounds. Those are created by the woman I am with, when they drink said cognac."

"Really?"

With a slight nod of his head, he leans in to tug on my lower lip just a bit with his teeth before he responds, "Surely, you don't doubt me."

At this very minute in time, there is a possibility that I might say anything which is why I simply smile.

Pulling away from me, he continues with, "Joking aside, I do have a decent wine cellar at my home over in Bicknell, if you're interested?"

Without a nanosecond to think, I answer, "Mr. Donovan, I am so interested."

Dade 303, Nash."

"Very good, sir."

Leaning in for another nibble on my lip, I have no doubt he is as turned on as I am. Even though, I am thoroughly enjoying this, I pull back.

With a small gleam in my eye, I continue, "in your wine that is." Oh my Lord, did I really just say that?

In a pretend grimace, at least I hope it is pretend, his response is very forward. "Well, Ms. Jensen, that is good to know." Nodding his head, "That it's my wine you are interested in. However, I must admit I am little disappointed."

"Oh, Mr. Donovan, I certainly didn't mean to disappoint you," I say as I look up at him in my best innocent look. Which I must admit actually isn't very good.

He continues, "I was hoping for a rousing game of sound."

"What? I really don't think I am up for any games. It has been a really long day. I would prefer to relax a little. If that is alright with you."

"Charli, it is perfectly fine with me. I just wonder if you have ever been introduced to the game?"

Looking into his eyes, I can barely find the words to answer but I manage to say, "No, I don't think so."

Flashing me a heart stopping smile, he begins. "In the game, their are two ways to win."

Rubbing my hands together, in a teasingly manner I add, "I like to win. That is one thing you will find about me, I am highly competitive."

"Good. The game is more challenging with competitive people. I must warn you, I am highly competitive myself."

With a slight nod, the old athlete from years gone by is beginning to emerge. I am thinking to myself, lookout Donovan you are going down.

Just as I am about to inquire about the rules of the game, we pull onto the travertine paved drive of the luxury apartment complex, Dade 303. Where the doorman is waiting to greet us. Hurriedly moving to open our door, Houston greets him with a generic smile, "Martin."

"Good evening, Mr. Donovan, Mam."

Between Martin, the luxurious fountained lobby, and the overall ambiance of the building, I wouldn't have been surprised to find a uniformed elevator operator standing at the ready, when the doors opened. Instead Houston, inserted a key card into a slot, which zips us up toward the twentieth floor. On the ride up, I feel the warmth of Houston's hand as he rests it on my lower back. I'm tingling, almost as if I have touched a live, sparking wire. Maybe that is what Houston is to me, the spark to help me feel alive again.

"I need to spend about thirty minutes making some calls since I was unexpectedly out of the office this afternoon."

"Oh really? Unexpectedly, out of the office." I glance up at Houston out of the corner of my eye, as I silently question myself, what in the world am I doing? Which initiates an internal conversation between my Midwest upbringing and my big city girl self. I'm living that's what I am doing. Even though this is not the way I envisioned this evening going, it has been memorable, so far, to say the very least. I was supposed to be at Chester's laughing enjoying a girl's night. Girl's night? Heck who am I kidding, I prefer this tall, sexy hunk beside me to the girls. I am most definitely enjoying this night. My heart is racing. My mid-west girl tries to give me some grief as the elevator stops. I think about just not getting out. What would he say if I just let the doors close with me inside and returned to the ground floor? Would that be the end of whatever this thing between us might become? Stop it! You are here for a glass or two of wine and some good conversation, nothing else. Yeah, right!

The elevator doors open providing an uninterrupted ocean view that is nothing less than spectacular. "Oh my. I knew it would be stunning but this is beyond stunning." I whisper.

With just a hint of amusement in his voice, he said, "I am going to make those calls. Make yourself at home."

Nodding, I enter the main living space feeling as if I am floating on air. It isn't that we're that high, it is the wall of glass ahead of me. If I didn't know better, I would think that the wall was actually missing. As if I have lost all control, my body automatically moves to it, like a moth being drawn to a flame. Standing motionless, staring out into the movement of the vast aquamarine waters Miami is known for I realize that my calm before the storm feeling is lost. Actually, the calm isn't lost just the storm. I really can't remember when the storm feeling wasn't there. Raising my eyebrows just a little, I question myself asking if I want this storm to dissolve. From the way I am feeling at this moment, it definitely isn't a storm. It is more like a full force hurricane with gale winds, moving through my body.

After a period of time, I turn to take in the beauty of the room. The honey earth tones of the furniture complementing a cream marble flooring that's covered with a plush, navy rug. It's a perfect space. As I stand absorbing the beauty of it, I realize I wouldn't change one thing. Everything portrays a calm and serene atmosphere that doesn't detract from the view. A view that I can't seem to get enough of; as I glance back to take another peek at those beautiful blue waters, I feel as if maybe I am getting a peek into Heaven. Drawing away from the outdoor view, I return to the penthouse. As my eyes sweep the room, I find myself moving toward the most magnificent piece I have ever seen. Slowly, reaching out to touch it, I almost withdraw my hand afraid that maybe I shouldn't. As if my hand has a will of it's on, it moves to touch Houston's chiseled face, which bears the beginning of a five o'clock shadow. These tiny prickles launch a sensation through me that is indescribable. With our eyes locked, all I can say is, "It is beautiful here."

"Yes, I do have a great view of the Atlantic."

Smiling, I agree that is beautiful, too. "I suppose beautiful isn't the appropriate word for describing the center of my attention. Maybe strikingly handsome would be more appropriate."

Breaking the spell, he cleared his throat. Looking down he continues, "Please forgive me for changing out of my suit. While I was on the phone, I knocked over a bottle of what smelled like some type of cleaner that the service must have mistakenly left sitting out." Smiling wickedly he continues, "I would be happy to get you out of your work clothes also."

Lightly slapping his firm, well defined chest, (I like doing that. Gives me an opportunity to touch all that sexiness) "I just bet you would." Running my eyes up and down I manage to get out, "You look as if you are comfortable in your jeans. I'm fine really." I thought he looked yummy before but mercy those jeans! They look as if they were made specifically for him. The way they hug his thighs, sitting low on his hips. Not to mention the white t-shirt that is topping them off.

"Let me show you around," as he spreads his arm wide welcoming me into the remainder of his home. We'll go upstairs in a minute. He leads me into a contemporary kitchen that has me drooling. I imagine most chefs would probably kill for it. Walking over to the island, I notice it has a unique countertop. He opens a drawer and pushes a button. Running my hand across the counter I ask, "What is this countertop?"

"That's Pyro lave." He tells me.

"Never heard of it. It's interesting."

"It's a volcanic stone. I had it shipped from Central France."

"So, you cook?"

"Not me, no. Why?"

"I just thought if you went to all that trouble to have something shipped that far, it must be for something you like to do. You know something special." I was so enthralled with the counter that when I looked up, he was gone.

"Houston?"

"In here."

I followed his voice and stopped at the entrance of a small room with rows and rows of wines. "Holy cow! You said a small wine cellar. There is nothing small about this."

"Ah, here it is." He returns with a bottle in hand. Handling the corkscrew with the precision of a surgeon welding a scalpel, he opens the bottle with expertise. "Let's allow it to breathe, shall we?"

He shows me the remaining rooms on this floor, including two bedrooms, three bathrooms, and his office-which I noticed was locked. Raising my eyebrows, "Trust issues?"

"Old habits, Charli. Just old habits. When you grow up with a mother that remarries ever five or six years, you learn to keep private things private. The locked door has nothing to do with you. I keep it locked always. Cleaning people, entertaining."

"Ah, yeah, because the cleaning people you employ are not trustworthy. I get it."

Shaking his head, "I don't employ a household staff at any of my residences except for my New York home.

"Pardon my asking but how many homes do you have?"

As we move upstairs he offers, "You know, it differs some years. It depends on where I am currently doing business, how long my stay requires. If I am opening an office in the region, I generally purchase a place. When I purchase, one of the qualifications for me to view a space, is the amenities. I rely on the building management to provide the services."

Nodding my head, just about all I can manage to say is "Well, alright then."

Let's see, right now my penthouse in New York City (which is my main home), here, hunting lodge upstate Michigan, Ski Chalet Breckenridge Colorado, beachfront just south of Los Angeles. So, here in the United States, five."

My confused look must have been funny to him because he laughed. "Something funny, Mr. Donovan?"

With a grimace, he replies, "No nothing is funny. I was just thinking about what your response to my New York place would be. So we are back to Mr. Donovan? I thought you would be more versed in proper etiquette."

"Pardon me. Proper etiquette? (The mid-west girl is about to break through.) Do you serve on the etiquette police board or something?"

Jokingly he continues, "Well, it's complicated Ms. Jensen. I happen to be familiar with a little known etiquette rule which deals with titles/surnames. I would have thought my little gift to you might have covered it."

OK, so I'll play along. Smiling, I say, " Well, I didn't get through the entire book. I was focused on so many of the rules that I actually feel asleep. By all means, please explain what this complicated etiquette rule concerning titles/surnames is?"

"The specific wording has slipped my mind but I do know it addresses attire."

Nodding my head, I say, "Sounds interesting. By all means, tell me some more about this little known attire rule."

Taking a step toward me, he responds with, "If one conversation participant is dressed in denim then both parties should be in denim or casual attire.

Part two of the rule address the usage of surnames when in such relaxed attire."

Crossing my arms and leaning back against a door that leads to some undisclosed room, I smile pretending to be upset when I say, "Really? Just what would that rule be that apparently my Mother, God Bless Her, failed to teach me?"

"It states two things: one: No person should be addressed by Mr. or Ms. If they are in denim, in their home, after nine pm. I am shocked that you are not familiar with that rule."

Shaking my head, I continue on, "Nope, afraid not. Never heard of it." Holding up my index finger, I add, "Here's the catch to that rule, I'm not at home." Smiling, I keep going, "So according to your rule, I should be addressed as Ms."

Seeing the folly in his made-up rule, he quickly adds, "As I agree you aren't but I am. No Mr. or Ms."

The second part of the rule addresses what? Pray tell me kind sir."

"I've forgot the actual wording but it does require that both conversation participants be in comfortable, relaxed clothing." He says as he takes a step narrowing the small space already between us.

"Well, since I don't have anything except the clothes on my back (as my Nonie would say) you might as well call the comfortable attire police. They'll have to cuff me and take me away."

With a mischievous smile, Houston leans into me, raises my hands above my head and holds them there while he grazes my lips with a kiss. Pulling back enough to lean his head in to whisper in my ear, "Cuff you? Sounds interesting but you can rest assured Charli that if you are cuffed in this house in any way, I will be doing the cuffing. No one will be taking you away physically. I wouldn't mind taking you mentally to a place called Pleasure Island." Nibbling on my ear with just enough pressure for me to barely feel his teeth he questions at just above a whisper, "Do you like handcuffs, Ms. Jensen?"

He asks as his hands hold me in that position just long enough to make me want more than the subtle kisses I am getting. Pushing my body to meet his, I can feel how hard he is becoming. The amount of heat building in my core is causing my city girl attitude to step up. I wouldn't object if he rammed himself into me as deep as possible this very moment.

Breaking away from me with a smile that tells, he knows exactly what he is doing, a moan escapes my lips. He says, "Ah, let the game begin."

Before I can ask if he is talking about sound, he continues with what I thought was the tour. Stopping just outside a door, Houston smiles at me, saying "Come with me."

As we enter a bedroom that has a view which mirrors what I saw downstairs, Houston simply says, "The master bedroom."

My eyes travel around the room landing on one of the most luxurious beds I have ever seen. The white comforter looks more like a cloud than a bed covering. I open my mouth but before I can make any comment, he touches my lips with his index finger.

"Not a word. When I take you on this bed it won't be because I have tricked you into this room. It will be because you want to be here in my bed. Make no mistake about that."

Jokingly, I press my lips together and wrinkle my brow trying really hard to not speak. My mind is running through all the possible ways in which I could end up in this bed. I quickly return to the one where I simply fling myself down onto it this very moment. Following Houston, we turn away from the object of my fantasy as he leads me into a closet that is about the size of my entire apartment. This room, because it is more than a closet, has all of his clothes hanging organized in a boutique style.

I stand taking it all in, "I thought I was fanatical about my clothes but you certainly have me beat."

Laughing all he says is, "I just like organization." Then he shrugged his shoulders adding, "I move between my homes often. You have no idea how helpful it is for my clothes to be in a particular order."

Turning 360° to absorb it all, "So let me get this straight, you have a closet like this in all your homes?"

Walking over to a leather covered bench he sits down, "No, not exactly like this but very similar. Some of the wood is different. I don't know what else but the layout is the same. My clothes are all arranged in the same order."

"I have heard of men like you."

"What kind of man would that be? I thought there was only one of me."

For lack of a better description I say, "A clothes horse. That's what kind." Looking around, I say, "A very organized clothes horse."

"A clothes horse?" Nodding his head, he continues. "I've been called worse. Much worse."

Pointing to a cabinet in the middle of the room, he continues, "See that remote?"

"Yes, oh my God you have a remote in your closet. You men and your remotes."

With a half smile he replies, "Yes, we do love our remotes. Push twelve."

I do as I am instructed. To the left, under his row of hanging t-shirts, a drawer opens. I look from the drawer to him and all I can say is, "You've got to be kidding me?"

I move over to it. In front of me are rows of neatly folded sweatpants in a vast array of colors. As I run my fingers over them, I tilt my head, just a little when I realize just how soft they are. I am trying to imagine him in a pair of these. I must admit, I am having some difficulty with that picture. He is not a man that I would expect to be in anything comfortable or slouchy. He seems to always be so well put together. Looking around to him, I ask, "Are you sure you don't mind?" With a small grin I continue, "Right now, I must admit these do sound pretty good."

"If I minded, I wouldn't have offered. You will find they are adjustable with the string. Please select a shirt as well." After making my selection, Houston leads me through a door hidden in the panel of the closet. Ok, I thought the closet was big, this is the bathroom every woman has secretly dreamed of.

"I'll wait in the bedroom." Looking over at me quickly, he adds, "Unless, you think my assistance is required. I will be happy to help in any way."

Not being able to resist this opportunity, I run my hand up his firm chest, smile what I hope is a seductive smile, lean into him and say, "I just bet you would."

Placing his hand on top of mine, he replies, "Baby, you have no idea."

Turning, he exits through a different door across the room. I quickly change not taking the time to look at this drool worthy bathroom since I want to get back to Houston. Ok, I must admit I salivated over the kitchen as well as the view. Who am I kidding? This bathroom is every woman's dream. The soaker tub is not like anything else I have ever seen. Exhaling deeply, I decide I might have to secretly label this place "the palace."

Quickly changing, into the softest warmup pants I have ever felt, I laugh just a little when I notice the length. Thank goodness they have elastic at the bottom. I attempt to roll them up just a little. The shirt I selected is large on me as well. I quickly gather the bottom into a knot. Looking at myself in the mirror, I almost laugh. I look like a rag-a-muffin. This is not exactly the picture I want to present to him but with a shrug of my shoulders, I enter the bedroom. I notice Houston is just laying his phone down on a table. Looking him directly in the eyes, I manage to say, "Don't you dare say a word." Moving my hands up and down, I continue, "This is as good as it gets."

Smiling almost wickedly, he says, " Baby, you look damn fine to me. I am sure that I will keep a mental picture of the way you look in my clothes for quite some time." Turning toward the door, he says "I think that our wine should be ready by now, shall we?"

Returning downstairs, the conversation turns to this magnificent home. "This isn't my home. I only stay here when I am in town, which is a good amount of time. I consider my place in New York as my home." Handing me my glass of wine, we gravitate to the outside to the verandah. Sitting in solitude with

Houston, unwinding and enjoying a glass of wine somehow feels right. I can't stop saying that. Glancing over at this striking, impressive man, I take a moment to reflect on how my life is progressing. Ten years ago, forget ten not even five years ago I would not have thought this possible. I remember my promise I made to myself all those years ago, to not slip back into the shell of a woman I was back then. Sighing softly, I take another drink and stand. Houston looks at me beginning to stand.

I shake my head no, as I walk over to him, gently putting my hand on his shoulder pushing him back into his seat. I sit my glass down, take his and place it next to mine. Our eyes never break contact. I swallow hard finding my courage. He seems at a loss for words when I straddle his lap. His eyes open wide and a small moan escapes his lips. Smiling seductively as I take his face in my hands, I lean in and kiss him as if there is no tomorrow. It's an emotional kiss, fueled by desire that leaves no question as to where I want this night to end. Through our deep kiss he mumbles against my lips, "Charli."

He pulls back ever so slightly and I can't help the Cheshire cat smile across my face. Houston mumbles in a husky tone, "Can you feel what you are doing to me?" Taking advantage of the fact that my very core is pressed against him, I move into his erection, gently but with enough force for him to feel the sensation through his jeans. Wrapping his hands around my waist, he leans back away from me just enough to look me in the eyes. What I see in his eyes mirrors my own, I am sure. What I see is desire. Pure raw desire. Our lips fuse together in a fiery, demanding kiss that represents our wanton need for more.

Grasping the back of my legs, this strong magnificent man stands, laying me on my back. As my head tilts backwards, Houston begins a slow assault on my neck causing my body to rise up to meet his. Raising my arms gives him the opportunity to slide my shirt off. His eyes travel from the rolled up band of the warm-up pants across my relatively flat stomach to my bra covered breasts. His strong hands follow the same path his eyes took stopping with them cupping the sides of each of my breasts. "You are beautiful, Charli."

"Houston, I want to see you also." Reaching down, he slowly removes his shirt, uncovering a muscular chest, causing my heart to race, my temperature to rise and molten waves of desire to flood my being.

Chapter 10

As I walk into the office, Joan looks up, gives me a small grin and returns to work. I make my way to my office quietly.

"CHARLI."

Darn, I wince and turn around and head back into Lana's office. "Thought you were going to get by me? Not really a walk of shame my friend but yeah I guess it sort of is," she says with a smile. "This brings back memories."

"The only thing I can say is … well, nothing really. It does give me some flashbacks but not all those walks of shame were mine if I remember correctly." I grin and raise my eyebrows a couple of times. "Hey, what's the point in working for yourself if you can't ever come in a teeny bit late?"

"Not sure two hours is a teeny bit but you are right about the working for ourselves thing. I only have one question and I won't ask for details because well, I don't need a visual of you, him I wouldn't mind, but give it up and I expect the truth."

"Ok?"

"Was he as good as I imagined he would be?"

My eyes get really, really big. I bite my lower lip with my front teeth and smile.

"OH MY GOD! I know that look. Enough said."

Shrugging, I turn to head to my office when I pop back to Lana's door and casually reply, "A lady doesn't kiss and tell."

"Lady? Yeah right. You do remember how long I have known you don't you? Now get out of here, I have the Smithson Industries proposal to finish. I am happy you had a great night, you deserve it."

"Thanks," I say as I head out her door and into my office. Entering my office, I notice a small package marked fragile sitting in the middle of my desk. I set my bag down in my chair, pick up the curious package, and head back out to Joan.

What is this?" Turning it in my hand.

It's a fragile package, obviously Charli," with a hint of pretend cynicism. "Are we having a little difficulty with our eyesight this morning?"

"Ha! Ha! I would never have known that it is a package marked fragile. I guess our school system failed me because I can't read." Pausing for effect, I continue on, "Oh wait, it didn't fail me because, (stressing it out) I - can – read." Pointing to the words stamped on the package, "fragile." All joking aside, "Do you know where it came from? "

Shaking her head, Joan replies, "Seriously, I don't know. It came about thirty minutes before you got here. Have you ordered anything lately?"

"Hmm, no I don't think so." I walk back into my office, move my computer bag out of my chair and sit down still holding the curious package. Just as I am about to open it, Joan buzzes asking if I want to take a call from a man that won't give his name. Thinking about it for a nano second, I hope I know who it is and that he is playing some type of game. I must admit, his game of sound was interesting. Smiling, I remember the sounds that I made last night.

"Sure, why not?"

I set the package down grinning. I do wonder why wouldn't Houston call my cell? "Who knows with him?" My phone rings a couple of times, I don't want to seem eager. Smiling as I pick up the phone, "This is Charli." My smile fades quickly.

"Charli? What happened to Charlotte?"

I pause, not today. Why now is he calling? "She's dead." Trying to stop my heart from beating out of my chest, I inhale and hold my breath for just a minute. Finally, I exhale preparing myself mentally as if I am about to go into battle. After what I hoped had been a pause in which he could read the unspoken message, I don't want to hear your voice. I finally spoke.

"What do you want?" I attempt to ask in an emotionless voice.

"I was calling to see how you are doing? I was concerned about you."

With a bitter laugh I asked him, "Why? I haven't heard from you in what five or six years?"

"Charlotte, please."

106

Don't call me that. My name is Charli."
Turning my back to the room, I sat with a deadpan
stare focused on the wall.

"How did you get this number? I thought I
made it absolutely clear the last time we spoke that I
did not ever want to hear from you again. That part
of my life is over."

"Is it really important as to how I got your
number? Look Charlotte,"

Shutting my eyes, I remind him "I told you
she is dead. She died ten years ago. Why are you
insisting on calling me that?" I ask with a sneer that I
hope reached through the line allowing him to feel all
the hatred I have for him still.

"Ok, Charli, is it?"

"Yes."

"It took me a long time to find you. Especially
after you checked out of the hospital."

"Did you ever think that maybe I didn't want
to be found? Wasn't it bad enough that I was hunted
like a rabid animal for years by reporters as well as
lawyers?"

"Yes, that thought crossed my mind more than
once but I can't give up."

"If I've given up, I don't see why you can't.
You weren't there. You didn't hear the screams. Smell
what I did. Do you think I will ever be able to
forget?"

"No you are right, I wasn't there. I have no doubt you will never forget but I can't let it go. I simply can't. I've continued to work, searching for the reason."

Laughing with the only emotion I found when I heard his voice, bitterness, I ask him. "Not give up on it? Searching for the reason. Are you crazy? We both read the report. Just like we know the reason. Human error."

"Charli, do you really believe that? He wouldn't make that kind of mistake. We both know that."

"I don't know that at all. You weren't there I was."

"You are correct, I wasn't there. Don't you think I wish I had been?" Hearing the pain in his voice as he continues, "I was the one that taught him. Charlotte, my world changed that day forever."

"Charli. My name is Charli. In what alternate universe would you think my world didn't change that day? No matter how much I try not to because forgetting isn't an option for me, I remember." Taking a deep breath, not giving Phillip time to speak, I find the courage to carry on with what I must say. "Every time I see the scars or every time I have blinding headaches, I have to remember the day the world stood still for me. You have to give up searching and just accept it. I have."

"Charli, he was my life. I have nothing left."

"You think he wasn't my life? Philip, I lost four people that day. It has taken me ten years to find the place I'm in. For whatever reason, I lived. I was given a second chance at life. I'm happy. Why can't you just accept that I-am-happy? Yes, it's a different happy than what I imagined but to say the least, I'm happy. Please, don't ever call me again." I can feel the sadness creeping over me like a fog rising up from the lake back home on an early autumn morning.

"Phillip, please, just let him go. Let me go. Don't ever, ever call me again. I am not Charlotte. She died that day, too."

The phone is halfway to the cradle when I hear him, "I am sorry. Please forgive me." Hanging up, I just sit facing the wall with my back still to my desk. I begin jerking all over as all the sorrow takes control. After a few minutes, I turn my chair around, and close my eyes. As if I were a young girl back in school, I fold my arms on my desk, lay my head down and take a deep breath. The tears that I thought my eyes wouldn't cry begin. Foolishly, I had imagined that those tears had stopped a long time ago. I ask to my empty office, "Oh God! Oh God! Oh God! Why now?" I have no idea how long I sit that way but finally I stand, pick up my bag and walk out the front door without saying a word to anyone. Once I get outside into the bright Florida sunshine, the fog dissipates a little. Rather than going home, I go over to Coastal Park on Key Biscayne.

This is the place that represents what I thought Miami would be like when I first talked to Lana about starting Supreme Corporate Travel. I instruct the driver to drop me off at the South Entrance. I need to just escape by walking through the Park Gardens this will also give me an opportunity to think about Phillip's call. What I am going to do? The anniversary is coming soon. A decision must be made as to whether I am going to join forces with him or simply let it go. Looking around, I am happy this is a weekday morning with very few people here. I can just wander. Let my thoughts take over. When I leave today, my decision must be made.

Chapter 11

My phone has been vibrating about every fifteen minutes for the last two hours. I am not sure I want to know who is calling me. What I do want is to stay lost here a little longer in this old zoo site. Sometimes, I think I like it so much because of the decayed, empty cages. For a long time, I felt like I was an animal locked away in a cage. People around me were watching and waiting for me to react in some way to the accident. Little did they know, the way I responded to being broken physically as well as mentally was to simply sink into myself. That's how I've always handled things. I learned early to hide my actual feelings from my brothers. Lord knows they would give me grief over just about anything. I can't help but smile when I think of how simple life was back then. When my greatest decision was what clothes I would be wearing. I suppose that is the way it is with most people when they are in high school. Wandering the paths and watching for any wildlife that calls this place home helps me find tranquility. The peacocks are my favorite especially when they display their magnificent tail feathers.

Walking through The Gardens, looking at the empty cages, I have a calm but eerie feeling spread through my body. Sometimes that's the way I feel, empty. If I team with Phillip, I know I will have to relive the past yet once again. I am not sure that is something I want to go through but the nagging question that I can't seem to let go of is what if he is right? Suddenly, I don't want to be alone. My eyes grow wide with surprise when I take out my phone. "Oh crap!" I see fifteen missed calls from either Lana, Joan, or Houston. Easiest first is my motto. I chicken out by sending Lana a text.

Stop freaking. Am OK. Just needed some alone time. Will fill u n later.

Houston

Slamming my hand on the desk, I ask an empty room, "What in the hell am I doing?" Actually, I don't need anyone to supply an answer. I already know it. I should be re-reading this entire report not skimming the summary based on the Singapore Brief. Most people would think that I have nothing else to do today except worrying about Charli. I have blasted every person that has any connection to her. That woman is driving me crazy. Turning my chair away from the desk, I overlook the Miami skyline but what I see is a beautiful woman lying beneath me. Her eyes filled with lust and desire on the edge of satisfaction. What I hear is her voice husky with need, as she said, "Take me Houston." Charli Jensen is driving me crazy.

112

Our picture might have shown up in several news rags today which puts her face in front of hordes of people. If so, I have no idea what nut job might possibly have picked up on her. Nash needs to put a small detail together. I can already imagine how she will react to that. Maybe Jeff? He'd be good with her. Besides his wife would beat me to killing him if he so much as looked at her in a sexual way. Glancing at my titanium watch, I realize she has been out of touch for two hours at least, when my assistant buzzes to remind me my meeting will begin in the small conference room in five minutes.

Pushing back from my chair, it sinks in that this woman has taken me by storm. I can't remember a time that I have ever felt this way. Even though, I am more than concerned about her at this moment, the fact that she is in my life is actually amazing. She seems to understand just what I need when I need it. She stands toe to toe with me. I really like that she has absolutely no problem putting me in my place.

Charli

I'm really dreading this because none of Houston's communication has been through a text but all calls. I enter the numbers, push send and almost before I can get the phone to my ear, someone answers.

"Mr. Donovan's phone, Melinda speaking."

"Ah, this is Charli Jensen and I was trying to get in touch with Houston, I mean Mr. Donovan."

"Oh yes, Ms. Jensen, I'm Mr. Donovan's Miami assistant. He is in a meeting at the moment but I was given strict instructions to pull him out if you called. Mam, I know we have never met and please forgive my forwardness but are you alright?"

"Yes, yes I'm fine. Thank you. Why?"

"Mam before Mr. Donovan went into the meeting, I was told to call your number every fifteen minutes until someone answered."

This little tidbit of information unsettles me. Squeezing my eyes shut, I can only imagine what he will say to me. "Oh, ok. I really hate to pull him out of a meeting. Why don't you just slip him a message that I called. He can return my call then."

"Ms. Jensen, please forgive me for saying so but I want to keep my job. Can you hold while I get him? Please, Ms. Jensen."

"Yes, I'll wait." Good gracious, that woman sure said please enough. I can't imagine Houston being that upset because I didn't want him pulled from a meeting.

Answering the phone as briskly as I have ever heard him, "Charli, did something happen? Where are you? Who was the call from?"

"Well, hello to you, too. Houston, I'm fine. I'm out on Key Biscayne at Coastal Park." How did you know I had a phone call?

"Coastal Park, Key Biscayne." I will send Nash to pick you up."

"Houston, that is so kind of you but don't send Nash. I will call a cab.

"Charli, this is not up for discussion. I have been concerned about you to say the least."

"Ok, then thank you for sending Nash. Hey, how did you know I left the office?"

"I called your phone. You didn't answer so I called your office. Joan explained, saying you left right after you got an upsetting phone call. Neither Lana nor Joan knew where you were. I was concerned that something had happened to you."

"Something did happen to me but it isn't the way you are thinking. Joan was correct in that the phone call upset me. I needed to get out of the office to be able to process the conversation I had just had. I found this old abandoned zoo site not long after I moved here, it's crazy I know but this place is calming to me. I needed to think about some very personal things so I came here to do it."

Chapter 12

When I finally wander to the parking lot, there is that familiar navy Audi SUV parked in a place of prominence. It wouldn't matter if it was parked in the front or the back of the lot. With Nash sporting dark sunglass, hand over hand standing beside the rear door, an aura of prominence is present. Walking toward the SUV, he opens the door with a very cool welcoming.

"Mam."

Crap, crap, crap! If that emotionless tone is his response, I can only imagine what Houston's will be. I think a part of me really hoped to find a six foot four surprise in the back of the SUV. Oh well, I've learned to live with disappointments.

Sitting in the back of this vehicle now makes me think of how Houston waylaid me outside my office. I can't help but focus on the wave of excitement I really felt when I saw him, waiting. That's one little morsel of information I think I'll keep to myself.

Leaning forward just a little, I say, "Thank you for picking me up. I hope you didn't have any problems getting here."

"You are more than welcome. Today is actually the first time I've been to The Gardens but I didn't have any trouble. Do you go there often?"

"No, Not really. I actually found the place by mistake one day after I'd lived here about a month. Because of my love for animals I thought this was a small petting zoo type place." With a shrug of my shoulders, my explanation continues, "I really don't know what made me think that. Doesn't really matter though. Listen, I am sorry for causing you any problems or messing with your schedule today."

"Ms. Jensen, picking you up wasn't the problem. It is fine. Every morning, I check my schedule but it takes many turns throughout the day. Houston, seems to always change it some way so rarely does it end like it was scheduled at the beginning of the day."

Clearing my throat, I find the courage to ask, "You said picking me up wasn't the problem. What was the problem or do I have to ask?"

Looking at me through the mirror, was enough of an answer. I knew the problem came with chocolate hair.

"Nash, can I ask you something else?"

"Yes, Mam, ask away."

Looking out the window, as we pass by other vehicles, I wonder, "Will you answer it truthfully?"

"Honestly Mam, it depends on what you ask. There are some things I am not at liberty to discuss," not exactly what I was expecting but it's the response I get. As I glance up at him, I notice he's looking back in the mirror quite a lot. (Wow, what driving skills.)

"That's fair enough but I think you can discuss what I am going to ask."

"I notice you call Houston, Houston and everyone else calls him Mr. Donovan."

"Yes, Mam. I do."

"Would you stop it with the Mam business? You can't be that be that much older than me."

"No, Mam. I don't think I am but if it is all the same to you, I prefer the Mam."

There it is, that icy tone. I really have no idea why it should shock me since I was actually expecting it. It is different to expect it than it is to actually get that tone. "Well, whatever makes you happy, I suppose."

With a little bit of a cough, Nash quickly responds, "It doesn't matter what makes me happy, it's what makes Houston happy."

Smiling just a little, it's good to know that Houston prefers Nash call me Mam. Well, Mam it is then. Back to my question, "Why do you get to call him Houston? It's none of my business. I just wondered." Sitting back quietly, I wait for his answer.

With the biggest grin, he began. "It was supposed to be my sophomore year at college but I had failed several classes my freshman year. I wasn't sure college was for me but I had gone back with a promise to my Mama to try harder. You know that old saying if Mama isn't happy, nobody's happy?"

"Yes, I know it." (If only I could make a promise to my Mama.) There was this guy on the opposite end of my floor that seemed to have it all. You know looks, grades, girls, money and friends."

"I know the type. Let me guess, that was Houston?"

"Yes, it was. One day, I saw him with another one of his visitors. Well, it wasn't but about 15 minutes till I saw another girl standing outside his door, just about ready to knock. I'd seen this happen a couple of times with him. It didn't really bother me. Only this time, the girl in the hall was one that I was interested in. So, to make a long story short, I saved her from getting her feelings hurt." Laughing, he went on, being the egotistical ass that he is/was, Houston thought I did it for him. One thing led to another and we've been saving each other in one way or another ever since."

Not what I was expecting. "Ok, I have to ask, how it went with the girl."

"We dated for two years."

Wanting to hear more I ask, "So you have been with him since you graduated?"

Shaking his head, "No. I realized school wasn't for me. So, I did a couple of tours in the Middle East. I ran into him at a veteran's celebration back at school that his company was sponsoring. He needed somebody he could trust. I needed a job."

Pulling into my building's parking lot, I grunt just a little.

"Is something wrong, Mam?"

"No, I was just thinking that this building isn't exactly Dade 303."

"No, Mam but very few buildings are like Dade 303. Correct me if I am wrong but your company is young. Just because you are starting here doesn't mean you'll stay here. Even if you do, stay here that is, there is nothing wrong with it. Lots of people have a whole lot less."

"I suppose you're right about that, Nash. I should be thankful for having a roof over my head. I am also thankful that you picked me up and we had an opportunity to talk." As I reach over to put my hand on the door handle, Nash exits the SUV. Before, I can get out he is around it and holding the door open for me.

Flashing him a half smile, I say, "Thanks again for rescuing me but I'm really not sure what all the fuss was about." I walk away from the vehicle shaking my head. I get about three steps when I stop, turn and see Nash walking behind me reminding me of a puppy I had when I was little. The way it followed me everywhere taking every step I took. Looking at him, I put my hands on my hips and ask, "What are you doing?"

"I am to make sure you get inside and that you are ok," he replies in a kind, patient voice.

"In case you haven't noticed, I am a big girl and I really don't need you to do that. You can see I am fine." Turning, pointing at the door of my building, "I am going in through that door, across the lobby, up in the elevator, down the hall and into my apartment. Then, I am going to lie down on my bed and forget this day. Now, does it sound like I need you to walk me? I am fine. I promise you."

Lifting his eyebrow to create that curious look of his, Nash replied, "Mam. I am under strict instructions. Let's just go inside and we can discuss it in there."

Mumbling under my breath, I agree and walk on. As quick as we get into the lobby, I take my phone out of my bag and text Houston.

U have got 2 b kidding?

I waited a minute, Houston didn't answer. Looking at Nash, I said, "He'll never know. You can just go but he kept walking with me.

Nash reached into his pocket, pulled out his phone. Read a message then looked at me. My phone went off.

In what realm do you think this would be a joke?

All the way into my apartment? I AM FINE.

Are you shouting at me?

No, just trying to make a point. He doesn't have to go up.

Yes he does. Humor me.

I turn, look at Nash, "Well come on since I know you are coming no matter what I say." Rolling my eyes with exasperation, I walk off and punch the elevator button.

"Yes Mam, I am. We both knew that from the beginning, if you excuse my saying so." Stopping, I glance around over my shoulder and give him my death defying stare. "Your right. Now comes the search and destroy," as I hold my up my leather cross body tote.

Looking at me as if I had gone crazy, I roll my eyes. "Obviously, Nash you are not married or deal with many females."

"No, Mam. No females around."

That does it! I stop dead in my tracks and look at him. "Nash, it is none of my business, if the answer is yes, it is fine with me but after that comment I just have to ask."

"Yes, Mam. Ask away."

"Are you gay?"

Standing with his hands behind his back and a deadpan look on his face, he answer, "No, Mam. I am not."

Waving my hands around for no particular reason other than just to move them, I look Nash in the eye and point blank ask, "So, let me get this straight, there is no special someone or Mrs. Nash?"

"No, Mam. No Mrs. Nash."

"OK, now my search and destroy mission." Looking at me as if I had grown another head, I held up my bag. "Just watch. I search in my bag for my keys. Then by the time I have found them, my bag is destroyed. See search and destroy?"

Laughing and shaking his head, "Women."

I am about to unlock the door when he holds out his hand, "Mam, keys please"

I roll my eyes, "You are killing me."

He unlocks the door and we enter. Before, I can close it he is on the phone. No doubt it's with Houston. I walk over to the counter and put my bag down. Closing my eyes, I mumble, "My laptop bag. Oh shit! Oh shit!"

Nash turns, looks at me and says, "Yes, sir. She is all safe and sound in her apartment. Just a moment sir. Ms. Jensen, is there something wrong?" Nash asks giving me a quizzical look.

As I motion to him, "Go ahead and I'll tell you when you are off the phone." Shaking his head, "No, Mam. Houston heard you. He wants to know what is wrong."

As I cross over to lay my bag on the table/desk, I pick up my phone to text both Lana and Joan.

"Things are alright. She is fine. She has misplaced something. Yes, I will check in when I return." Clicking off his phone and putting it away, he walked a little closer and stopped by my sofa.

"Nash, I have done something incredibly stupid."

"Other than disappearing for several hours?" Crossing the remainder of the room to me with his emotionless face, "Tell me what you think is so incredibly stupid."

"I've lost my laptop." Throwing my hands in the air and walking around my dining table, my rant begins. (my city girl attitude takes over) "Well, that is just the icing on today's little cake, isn't it?" Stopping behind an end chair, I peck on the back of it with my fingernail. "I must have left the bag in the taxi when I was getting out at Coastal Park." And I'm off again with the circling the table. I say more to myself than to Nash, "How in the world could I have been so stupid?"

"First off, you are not stupid, Mam." Touching my arm, to stop my pacing, "Let me discuss this with Houston. Then, I will take care of it."

I look at him in disbelief. "Take care of it? How in this world will you take care of it?" Actually, that phrase hits a nerve. I turn on him, "I know you are trying to help but take care of it. What does that mean? Does that mean you'll talk it over with Houston about the idiotic thing the little woman has done? Not that I'm actually his little woman. Does that mean Houston will send you to buy me another laptop? Cause, buying another one will not exactly make all my problems go away. Does that mean you'll find mine?" Looking at him with what I am sure is my Midwest girl's redneck death ray glare, a strange look comes across his face.

Holding his hands up in defense he says, "Well alright. Let's forget Houston. Tell me all you can remember about the taxi, the color, anything you can remember about the driver."

"Do you think I will get it back?"

Nash grimaced, "Frankly Mam, I don't know but I will do all I can to help you. That is what you want, right? Me to help you?"

Just a little embarrassed by my tirade, I bite on my lower lip and then give him a big hug that I'm sure made him very uncomfortable.

"Yes, Nash that is exactly what I want. I don't know what just happened or why I went off on you but I am sorry. I usually reserve that level of going ballistic for my brothers. Please forgive me."

Returning my smile, he assures me, "There is nothing to forgive. Remember, he is expecting your call. Take my advice, call him right after I close the door."

Chapter 13

Talking to Houston, helped me feel better. It's not that I need a man but if I am going to have one in my life why shouldn't he more delicious than Swiss chocolate. I couldn't or rather wouldn't tell him specifics about the call. It was just too personal. I don't want anyone to know. I am sure Joan told Lana about it and the way I suddenly disappeared from the office. What am I thinking, of course they both know they were involved in the calling frenzy.

Houston will be by after work. I know he said in a text earlier today that he wouldn't get out of his office until around seven. That means he won't be here before seven forty-five at the earliest. I think I'm just going to lie down for just a few minutes. After this morning and not a lot of sleep last night, I could use a nap.

Smiling about last night, I can't believe that really happened. As I drifted off to sleep, I think about the night and the gentle touch he had. It was as if, I was having the perfect sexual experience. The way I had always imagined the movie kind portrayed. A generous lover that put my needs first, Houston was just that. Even when he scooped me up, like he was handling a wounded bird that needed tenderness, and carried me up the steps to his bedroom.

Laying me down on that luxurious comforter, Houston bent over me, speaking between kisses,

"Charli ... you... are... so ... beautiful. ...Let... me ...love...you," moving his way up my stomach. I tried to hold back the moan that desperately wanted to escape my lips. Giving in to the desire that was building, I allowed myself a one word reply, "Yes." Stopping on one of my scars, "What's this my beauty? How did you hurt yourself?"

"Just an accident, a long time ago."

"I can't make it go away but I can kiss the memory away for a while." His tongue traced its outline and moved upward. Cupping my breast, he gently squeezed just enough for me to want more.

Houston

Standing in what some prefer to call a power stance, I have no doubt my facial expression is fierce. With my arms are crossed, I am flexing the muscles in my back looking out the wall of windows like a lone wolf watches over the desert. Most of my business associates would agree with my description. Actually, rumor has it that some describe me as a wolf in the boardroom. A great many women would concur that my alpha male instinct carries over into the bedroom.

On this night, one of the few differences between me and a wolf is the wolf would see the array of lights flickering in the night sky in front of him. I am focused on one thing or rather one person when Nash enters the office. Without turning, I manage to calmly ask, "What did she say?"

"Nothing much, sir. As a matter of fact, after I picked her up she acted as if everything was normal. She seemed fine. I took her straight back to her apartment and as you know had just a little difficulty seeing her upstairs. After that was cleared up, she didn't seem upset until..."

"Until what?"

"Until she realized she had left her bag containing her laptop in the cab."

"What? That was what she lost? She lost her laptop?"

"Yes, that was what she lost."

"Is she really that scatter brained? This is the second time she has done that. Did you locate it?"

"Yes, sir. I was able to locate it."

"Quit the sir, crap. We are alone. You know how I feel about my best friend calling me sir."

"I know, Hugh. It's just sometimes, I forget."

Turning away from the window, I find Nash's facial expression unreadable, I stress once again, "The only time I ever want you to call me sir is when we are in some high level situation. I really don't care for it then but it completes the power imagine. Let's get back to Charli. Tell me about the bag."

"She did a pretty good job with the taxi description. Luckily, the driver was honest and reported it to the dispatcher. I picked it up, it's in my office waiting for you."

Returning, back to my view of the city, I toss out, "Thank you. I really don't know what I would do without you. You keep my world sane."

Laughing, Nash turns to leave the office, "Sane, yeah that is exactly what your world is."

"I will be ready to leave in about thirty minutes."

"Ok, let me know. I'll be in my office."

"Nash,"

"Yes."

"Find the bastard that upset her so. I want all the details down to what he ate for dinner last night."

"Already on it Hugh."

Turning to look at Nash, I smile. "I have no doubt."

Chapter 14

When Houston arrives later that evening, he has my laptop. "Oh thank goodness! Nash found it!" I threw my arms around him, giving him a thank you kiss that he won't forget for some time. Using his special people reading talent, he can sense that I don't want to discuss the day's events. He understands, I wanted to forget everything and simply relax.

We order delivery from a local Cuban restaurant. While we're waiting I offer, "Let me show you my home because it will take all of five seconds. You really don't have to move from the sofa for the tour. Just turn your head."

I stood up took five steps sweeping my hand in a grand gesture that any game show hostess would be proud of, "This is the kitchen, dining room/home office as you can tell by the mess." I step off another five steps, open a door, "bathroom," three steps more "bedroom," raising my eyes two or three times which made him laugh. "Finally, another five steps, I am back onto the sofa here beside you. See five seconds." We both laugh as I sit down beside him.

"Charli, your place is great besides it isn't the place I am here for," as he arches his eyebrows and smiles.

"Oh really? You mean you aren't here for the semi-hard couch and poor deck view? Then I have no idea what would bring you here."

"If I am not here for those things then let's see what I might be here for," leaning in closer to my lips he whispers "it's the executive level home office." Laughing, I pick up a pillow and bop him in the chest with it just as the doorbell rings.

"Sit here beautiful, I'll be right back. I'm just going to answer the door. I assume it is the food unless you are expecting someone."

"You most certainly will not! This is my home and you are my guest."

Well, yes, this is your home but I am not a man that is in the habit of having my meals purchased by a woman, beautiful and pouty faced or not."

"Houston Donovan, my guests do not pay for their meals, mister." Throwing up his hands he agrees, "I give up, okay, okay. This one time."

Since my dining room table is full of work, we sit on the sofa, eating out of carryout containers talking about the first time we each ate Cuban food. Agreeing that traditional Cuban coffee is either too strong or too sweet for us, we dig into the meal laughing and enjoying each other's company. I am not sure which I enjoy more, the food or knowing he seems to be comfortable here in my home. I am thoroughly embarrassed when I yawn once or twice.

"That is my signal, I better get going." As Houston leans over kissing my cheek, I turn to face him, prepared to ask him to stay with me in my humble abode as my eyes find pools of brown

131

focused on my face. Houston's lips meet mine causing me to slide my arms around his neck. He pulls me closer but not stopping with me beside him but up onto his lap. I can feel his strong sculpted thighs underneath me. As our kiss deepens, the need for Houston to be inside me grows. Pulling away and leaning our foreheads together, he says, "I really would like to stay but I have a conference call that I have to take from the office in approximately fifty minutes."

"Oh, it seems sort of late but okay."

"It isn't late if the people on the other end are in Melbourne, Australia. There is a twelve hour time difference."

"Oh yeah, I forgot you are Mr. Worldwide mogul, taking companies and making money."

Tilting his head as if he is thinking about that, "Hump, I suppose. Will I see you tomorrow?"

"I would like that," as I run my hand up his loosened silk tie, wrapping my left arm around his waist pulling us closer together.

"By the way before I go, I wanted to ask if you have had an opportunity to discuss the Black and Gold Gala with Lana?" Making a face, I shake my head. "No, but I will tomorrow. I promise."

"OK, beautiful."

"Not hardly."

Charli, I don't like it when you are negative about yourself. Yes you are, not up for discussion," leaning down to give me one more kiss before he leaves. I melt into him as if he is the sun and I am an icicle with moisture slowly dripping from me.

Charli

That smell what is it? It vaguely smells like hot metal. Why am I coughing? I hear something, it's sounds like something popping. I try to shake my head so it will clear. Where am I? I raise my head just a little, open my eyes and look around. OH NO! OH NO! Next thing I know it is black.

I sit straight up in my bed, jerk my head around and automatically know, it is the dream again. Who am I kidding, that dream is actually a nightmare. My heart is racing. I take deep breaths to try and slow it down. I lean toward the nightstand, pick up my cell phone. It's one in the morning I lay back down curling into a ball, afraid my real life nightmare will happen again.

Chapter 15

Hey Charli, want the usual?"

Nodding my head, "Sounds good to me Rose." Looking around the Java Hut, I ask, "Where is everybody? It's a little empty in here."

With a little shrug, Rose replies, "Don't look a gift horse in the mouth, sister. You're a little later than normal. That off to work rush is over." It's been a couple of days since you have been in, "Where have you been? I've missed your commentary on customers."

"I've been taking a different route to work."

"By the looks of that smile, I'd say a certain friend of mine that might be named Charli is enjoying these different routes."

Smiling, no doubt with a bit of a sheepish grin on my face, my only response is "maybe."

"So if that's the way you want to play it, then I'll accept the maybe answer today but just to give you a heads up, I will be expecting more detail in the future. So, I suppose if I ask how ya doing today, you're going to give me a basic uninformative answer."

Looking at Rose, I see a hit of a sparkle in her eye. She is really enjoying this. "You know, I am in a really good mood today. Thanks for noticing."

"Anytime my friend. Hey, you like basketball, don't you," Rose asks as she is returning to the counter with my coffee.

"I love it why? I played in high school and some intramural games at college."

"I've got an extra ticket for Thursday's game. My neighbor was going with me. He called me a few minutes ago telling me he can't make it."

"I would love to go, if you are asking."

"Course they are in the nosebleed section but hey it's a game."

"I'll have to tell my brothers and do the sisterly thing. Rub it in."

Shaking her head as if she was in amazement, "My brother could care less. He is a big old football fan. Yuck!" Putting her hand on her chin as if she was doing some type of intense concentration. "I do have to admit, I like the way those football uniforms fit those bodies," winking at me. We could make it a girl's night. I usually go to some type of after party, so don't come in jeans and a t-shirt."

Laughing, "Glad you told me about the party. I would have come in jeans. You obviously know me."

"Tipoff, is seven. Meet me outside the arena at six thirty." Turning to walk out the door, I say over my shoulder, "Sounds good. See ya then." The week moves by swiftly which surprises me. Usually, when I have some plans for the end of the week it drags on. These couple of days went just the opposite.

Houston has been swamped with work this week. I've only seen him once and that was briefly when he sent Nash to pick me up for lunch. The Miami office of Highland Diversified is being restructured or so he says. I have absolutely no idea what is required when one restructures an entire office but I assume it means someone or perhaps more than one person is losing their job. Wrinkling my brow, I sure hope no one is but if it must happen, I hope it is that rude man from the elevator.

Game day is finally here. Arriving at the arena before Rose, I am enjoying watching the variety of people that are entering. I've noticed quite a few stretch limos pulling into what appears to be a private entrance. Maybe the celebrities will be in attendance tonight. I suppose it depends on what is happening in South Beach. I hear Rose before I see her.

"Look out boys, the girl's hot tonight."

Turning just a little to my right, I see her moving toward me continuing to speak not allowing me to say a word, "Charli, WOW. That's about all I can say."

Smiling at her with a sheepish grin, "You said no jeans but I thought these white denim might be ok."

"Might be ok? Are you kidding? Girl, you have classy sexy written all over you."

"Ah, Rose did you see yourself before you walked out of your place? You are looking pretty H-O-T yourself."

"Charli, are those pumps Boutins?"

Laughing, I nod yes. "They cost me a fortune but I love the color. It isn't a true black but it's not an off black either." Let's head on in.

As we are making our way to our seats, which actually are not as bad as I anticipated, I have a collection of cards with names/street address/phone numbers on them. Having to really work at remaining calm, I elbow Rose asking, "What is up with men? I keep getting these cards with a name, address and phone number. What do they think I am?"

With a hint of laughter in her voice Rose explains, "Charli, those are your tickets into after parties. You have so much to learn about professional sports. Let me see what names you have and then we will discuss which ones we want to hit."

Handing my cards over to her, she says "Oh girl, these are some hot tickets. Let's sit down and I will tell you what I know about these or at least what I have heard about some of them because you have some invites here that lots of people would die for."

More than once during the game, the fan cam shows us on the jumbo Tron. This is fun! Our facial expressions have provided everyone with some laughs. The game has been close but at halftime Miami is up nine points. In professional basketball, that is nothing. Those nine can be scored in less than thirty seconds. Standing up to stretch, Rose and I are chatting with the people behind us. Suddenly, I see a familiar face moving toward me. Not meaning to be rude, I attempt to ignore his presence beside me by continuing my conversation.

Speaking as if I am standing alone, Nash says, "Ms. Jensen, he would like to see you."

Realizing my tactic isn't working, I acknowledge his presence by responding, "Well, good for him. Just because we had *some moments* that doesn't mean I am at his beck and call."

He maybe dressed casually but his mannerisms in no way reflect his surroundings as he continues, "No Ma'am it doesn't."

Turning to look Nash in the eye as much as it is possible for me since he is near Houston's height which puts him over six foot, I calmly state the obvious, "The game is getting ready to resume, I don't know what you are going to do but I am going to sit down, right here beside my friend." I look over at Rose. That's when, I decide I might have to scrape her off the floor. She seems to be melting as her eyes are taking in the full frontal experience of Nash with his strong facial features and muscular arms. Smiling, I look from one to the other as I introduce them. "Rose, this is Nash ah?"

"Nash will do Ma'am."

Well that is just interesting, only one name. "Rose this is Nash. Nash this is one of my best friends, Rose."

"Ma'am."

Good grief! Standing back as I witness the exchange in front of me, I realize he has that same quality that Houston has. It's what I secretly refer to as his, do you want to hop into bed with me, look. Those smoldering eyes. The hint of a smile. Nash has a dimple! I've never noticed that before.

"Oh, please call me Rose."

Just about that time the buzzer sounds signaling the beginning of the third quarter. Clearing my throat, I that Nash for stopping by and reminding him to give Houston my message.

Shaking his head, his only response is "Ma'am, be sure to check your phone."

The game is tied at the final buzzer of regulation play. We are going into overtime. Rose and I have compared our entry tickets/cards. Some are the same, some not. Mapping out a plan of where we were going for the after parties, the OT began. I am engrossed in the play on the court when Rose elbows me.

"Ah, Charli, you need to report to the scorer's table immediately.

"What?" The next thing I know during a timeout, I hear over the sound system, "May I have your attention please. A Charli Jensen is needed at the scorer's table immediately. Charli Jensen immediately report to the scorer's table." I sink down into my seat, bending my head, trying to cover my embarrassment.

"Hey, you need to go to the scorer's table," one of the guys from behind leaned down and told me. Asking Rose, "How does he know my name?" Her reply came with a finger pointing at the scoreboard, "Oh crap, Charli everybody knows who you are."

Looking up, there I am, which actually is no big deal, my picture has been on there a couple of times tonight but this time my name is underneath it. How in this world did they know that? Standing up, I begin walking. The timeout is over and the game play has resumed by the time I reach the security officer guarding the entrance to the floor. I shut my eyes. Standing there isn't Nash but Houston. He is laughing with everybody around him. As our eyes meet, he smiles. Somehow, I get the feeling the smile on his handsome face doesn't reflect what he is actually feeling.

He jokes with those around us, as we walk over to front row seats beside someone that looks vaguely familiar. Trying my very best to not stare, I think actually the person on the other side of Houston is the star of the latest action packed Hollywood blockbuster. Looking around casually, that is when I realize every person around us looks familiar. Trying not to be star struck but I see a tennis player that is always in the news, a supermodel, a woman that reminds me of a famous politician. The list goes on and on.

As Houston puts his arm around me, I lean in, grit my teeth and manage to ask, "Really? Little extreme don't you think?"

Through those sensual smiling lips comes, "Next time come with Nash." I feel my phone vibrate. Pulling it out, Houston looks over at me with a raised eyebrow.

"Really? Now you check your phone."

That's when I notice, I have four missed texts. Two from Houston, one from a number I don't recognize and Rose. I open Rose's. *OH MY GOD! Who is that?*

I close my eyes, count to five which is giving me an opportunity to think about my response. I hear the buzzer going off. The game is over. Before I understand what is occurring, I am being helped up by a laughing Houston. Somewhere off to the side, I hear "Damn man! You having to track'em down? Heard what you did, when you were supposed to be watching my fine skills on the floor." Houston leans into this man some call a basketball god and made some type of comment out of my earshot that causes them to laugh and slap each other on the back. Men!

Houston, holds his arm out to me, pulling me into his side and introduces me. The ball player looks down at me saying, "Here's the thing. If you get tired of this piece of work (nodding toward Houston) you just look me up." I stand there saying nothing just nodding not being able to actually form any words. I have watched this man play basketball since he was in college now here I am having a one sided conversation with him.

My phone vibrates, again. I look at it. Oh darn, it's Rose. I didn't text her back. Turning around, I find her in the crowd of people that is remaining. She's standing there, waiting for me to pick up. Sheepishly, I say "Hello."

"You have got to tell me who he is. Have you known him long? Why haven't I heard about him? Wait I have heard about him, I bet. Is he the reason for the different route in the mornings?"

Turning away from Houston, I talk into the phone. "Houston is his name. I haven't known him long. The man I introduced you to earlier is his driver. Yes to the other thing you ask me."

"You mean they come in sets? Oh sweet me, Charli. You have been holding out. Listen don't worry about the after party because looks like you're going to have your own. I've already text a couple of people that I usually go with to check if they are here. They are, so I am all good. Now, listen to me, Go take care of that fine piece of man standing beside you."

"I don't know what I am doing, Rose. Obviously, this wasn't in my plan. I'm sorry." Pretending to fan my face, "He is fine isn't he?"

"You have to ask? Don't be sorry. If I had that standing beside me, girl I'd be dragging him out of here."

I smile and wave. "Talk to you later."

Turning around, Houston was talking to a gentleman that I recognize as the owner of the team. They are engaged in what looks to be a serious conversation. I seize the opportunity, taking a selfie and send it to my brothers. Feeling pretty smug, I wait for responses. Neither came, but after I looked at the time I understand why. It is late by most people's standards. Deciding they are probably asleep, I put my phone into my bag. Houston wraps up his conversation and away we go out some private exit.

"Where's Nash?" I ask as we were exiting the arena.

"He left just before the overtime ended. Gone home, I suppose. Why? Do you need something?"

"I was just wondering. He's always with you besides I don't think he has the thing I need. Well, I suppose he has one but it isn't the one I need."

Leaning down sideways, he said, "He better not have the thing you need. I don't share. Believe it or not, I have a driver's license. I don't need Nash for everything."

"Oh really? Couldn't prove it by me."

Putting his arm around my shoulder, he pulls me into him. With what most would call, a bedroom voice he says, "Baby, I'll be more than happy to demonstrate my skills."

Stopping and taking a step away from me, his eyes slowly travel down my body with a passion that leaves me feeling scorched from his gaze. Smiling semi-wickedly, he moves his hand down to a very low spot on my back as we walk. He must have unlocked the car using his free hand. A sexy sleek sports car directly in front of us beeps. Opening the door for me, he lightly caresses the spot where his hand touch's my skin. This seemingly small gesture, becomes one of the sexiest actions I've experienced.

As we roar away from the arena, I realize this feels right. Me being with Houston. I don't need to ask what our destination is. It really doesn't matter. I haven't felt this way in a very long time, if ever. I decide to simply sit back and enjoy the ride. He pushes some buttons, and the crooning voice of Old Blue Eyes himself begin. That's when I know this is going to be some kind of night. Suddenly, I ache for the firmness of him. I reach out, placing my hand on his thigh. This touch soothes my need. His hand covers mine as we race off into the promise of a heat filled night. We remain this way until we pull into the garage at Dade 303. When I try to pull my hand back, Houston's hand clamps down on mine. We sit like this for just a second enjoying this simple yet complex connection.

Chapter 16

"Good Morning, Charli. It's starting out to be a great isn't it?"

"I guess, Lana. I'm not sure how great it is starting but it sure sounds like someone is having a good one. Any reason I should know? It wouldn't be connected to the good mood I noticed Terrance in when I stopped by the Java House this morning?"

Smiling at me, "Possibly." I always enjoy watching her at the beginning of a new romance. She has so many facial expressions. I turn around and look at Joan as she hands me a package marked fragile.

"Okay? Weird. Where did this come from, Joan?"

"Messenger brought it this morning. Did you ever open that other package from a couple of weeks ago?"

Exhaling deeply and squeezing my eyes shut, "No, I forgot it. I laid it over to the side and didn't think anything else about it. I'm not sure where it is exactly."

I walk into my office, deciding to open today's arrival first. Sitting down at my desk, Deja-vu hits me hard. Closing my eyes, I give myself a brief pep talk. Reaching over to my computer, I click on my favorite music app, find something to listen to. Just as, I pull out my box cutter to open the package an upbeat song that always makes me happy comes on.

I sing along softly, because that is the only way I would ever sing out loud in public even if I am in my office. I break the seal and what do I find? A box inside. Okay. I open that box and go through this process two more times. Really, how immature is this? I wonder is my friend Rose at the Java Hut playing a prank on me. This is about like something she would do. Finally, I pull out a small wooden chest. What in the world? The outer package was labeled fragile. This doesn't look fragile to me. I try to open it but it seems to be locked.

That is when I notice the ecru envelope. Opening it, I smile, the embossed card simply reads: *Bring the contents of the first package along with this to The Museum and Gardens of Biscayne tonight. Your driver will pick you up from your apartment at seven. H.*

Definitely not Rose. I look around my office for the first package finally finding it inside a drawer under some papers. I open it and inside is a chest that matches the other one but larger. I lift the chest out, take a deep breath, "Really?" I open this box to find a beautiful antique wine glass laying in a bed of midnight blue velvet again with a handwritten note enclosed. *Try not to shatter this one.*

Smiling, I pick up my phone, *C ... U... @ 7.*

"Charli, did you finish the Rowling and Peele travel package?" asks Lana as she comes into my office, sits down across from me. I shake my head just enough to clear away any thoughts about what is locked up in the small chest. "Huh? I'm sorry Lana what did you say?"

"Did you finish the Rowling and Peele itinerary?"

"Yes, believe it or not, I've already emailed it. Why?"

"Peele contacted me just now and "assured" me he hasn't received anything from Supreme Corporate Travel."

"Well, it might be because I sent it to his partner, William Rowling. I doubt if they even talk? It's no wonder that this retreat we have assembled is the final attempt to hold together a company that clearly needs to be dissolved. We're a corporate travel company specializing in retreats not miracles. I'll send it to Peele right now," as I turn to my desktop.

"Just keep the sarcasm in the office, even though I agree with you." Looking down at my desk as she stands Lana sees the larger chest. "Charli, this is beautiful. Is it new? Where did you get it?"

Looking up, I smile, "Open it."

She opened the box and sighed. "This is gorgeous, May I?" Nodding my head, Lana picked up the fragile stemware admiring the etchings. '"Charli, these are orchids."

"I know, isn't it stunning?"

"Ok, give it up where did you get this or do I even have to ask?"

With a smile, followed by a little lower lip biting, I shrug my shoulders, "Houston."

"I should've known. It is beautiful. You know I really don't go for that "vintage" stuff."

"Stop with the air quotes, that drives me crazy and you know it."

"I know. By the way, the glass is beautiful too." I ball up a paper and throw it. I can hear Lana laughing all the way back to her office.

Chapter 17

Leaving my apartment, I make sure to bring both packages. I feared for my emotional health if I left either behind. If I have learned anything about Mr. Houston Donovan these last few months, I know to be in my lobby at the designated time. Houston or whomever picks me up is always prompt. That is one thing that was never my strong suit. Punctuality. Actually, I have begun to plan on being ready at least ten minutes earlier than any time I'm given. That gives me just a hint of a leeway. Just as I exit my building, a sleek dark blue luxury sedan pulled up. I am surprised to find Nash isn't the driver. A man, perhaps a few years older than Nash, comes around opening my door. "Ma'am, I'm Jeffery and I will be your driver this evening."

"Thank you Jeffery."

As we speed down, I-95, I think about my life and how happy I am. If a fortune teller had predicted that I would have met a very wealthy man, fell in "something" with him, I would have belly laughed, as my brothers say, because I would have thought she was crazy. The pathway of life sure can take a great many turns, mine definitely has. Wow, who would have thought I would be where I am now?

My brothers. I sit and look out the window biting the inside of my cheek. I need to call both of them. It's been awhile since I have talked to either of them. I haven't received a text or an email, except for the text about me being at the ballgame. I suppose staying in touch isn't the Walker way. I think that would make Mama really sad to know that the three of us have grown so far apart over the years. It's not that we don't love each other, it's just we are in different places/stages in our life. Nope, I am not going to do this. I can easily make myself depressed. Turning my thoughts to the objects in my bag, I can't help but smile and wonder what this night holds.

One thing I definitely know about tonight is that it is starting off mysteriously. Obviously, Houston has put a great deal of thought into it. Getting lost in my own thoughts we arrive at our destination before I realize it. As Jeffery is turning into long the drive, I make a mental note to ask Houston how we can use this wonderful estate after hours. Whatever he does to ensure our privacy, I do hope he continues it. When we get this place to ourselves, I feel really special.

Lost in my thoughts again, I am startled as Jeffery stops, about mid-way up the tree lined drive. I look over to my left that is when I notice the shadow of a man stepping out from behind one huge, old tree. How strange! Moving toward the car, he opens the door and gets in. Before, I can say anything, Houston breaks into the biggest smile as he takes my hand pulling me onto his lap all in one swift movement. Smiling back, looking into his eyes, he cups the back of my head pulling me to him taking my mouth in a passionate kiss as my brain struggles to register, we are continuing up the drive. The driver stops in front of the main entrance and soundlessly exits the vehicle. Sitting lost in each other my hands move across his strong, well defined shoulders down his arms. I can't help but marvel at the contrast of the softness of his shirt against his firm body. Breaking our heated connection, he draws back saying, "Charli, you're going to have to get off my lap or we will never get out."

Moving into the seat beside Houston, I exhale deeply. "Would that be such a terrible thing?"

Flashing me a devilish grin, his response somewhat shocks me. "As much as I want you at this moment, I take all precautions to prevent my employees seeing me ravish my girlfriend."

Girlfriend," nodding my head. Interesting choice of words. I really didn't know what I was to him. "Am I your girlfriend?"

Turning his body more toward me, his reply makes me a very happy woman. "I certainly hope so. Do you consider me your boyfriend?"

"Honestly?"

Yes, honestly?"

"I am not really sure what I think of you as, you are many things to me. I definitely think I would call you my somebody but I think we are just a little too old to be girlfriend/boyfriend." Nodding his head in agreement, we exit the car.

Looking at the driver standing very discreetly some distance from the SUV, we walk toward him. We stop beside him allowing Houston to have a brief conversation with him.

"Jeffery, as always this is fine. I will let you know. Don't expect my call for several hours at the least."

"Very good sir."

We walk a little distance away, when we hear the driver, "Sir, Ms. Jensen" stopping we turn, realizing Jeffery is holding the cloth bag I had placed my chests in.

"Ms. Jensen, you left this bag."

I contain a chuckle because he looks funny standing there in a suit holding a black/pink paisley printed bag.

"Thank you, again, Jeffery."

"Yes, sir. No problem."

Looking over at me with those eyes that scream, I want you, Houston teasingly says, "Really Charli? One thing for you to bring, you almost leave it."

"I have you know it was two things besides I was distracted."

"Cheeky!" Swatting my behind and trying to appear as if he is mad, I take him by the arm, look up and bat my eyelashes in a very dramatic way. We laugh as we walk across the pathway.

"Where are we going?"

Nodding his head forward, he assures me "Just a little further up this path and you will see."

We are walking arm in arm, enjoying the beautiful surroundings. It is almost as if we were the only people in the world. For this moment in my mind, that's what we are- the only people in existence.

"Charli, do you trust me?"

"Yes, I told you, you're my somebody."

"Remind me later, we need to discuss what that means but for now, I want you to close your eyes."

Closing my eyes, my heart is beginning to race. The beating increases to rapid pace when I feel something soft and satiny go over my eyes, changing the darkness of my closed eyes to complete blackness, a blindfold. Raising my hands to my face, I feel the soft satin fabric. Thoughts begin tumbling through my mind. Wondering what will come next. Then it dawns on me, I really do trust him. I might have just said it a minute ago to him but it is a fact.

Suddenly, I feel a small gentle nibble on my neck. MMM. I have no doubt this is setting the tone for the remainder of the night when he pulls me back against him allowing me to feel the firmness of his body against mine. Snaking his arms around my waist, his hands slowly move up to cup my breasts. Lost in this moment, I lay my head back allowing my body to get lost in the silent assault. While a warm tinging sensation is spreading across me I can no longer contain the moan of pleasure I am experiencing, Houston whispers ever so softly, "Oh no, baby. Not yet."

Moving away from me he directs me, "Hold onto my arm. I want to lead you the remainder of the way. I won't let you bump or hit anything."

Right now, he could lead me just about anywhere. The man knows how to use his hands that is for sure. Exhaling slowly, I nod my head in agreement. We are moving slowly with Houston guiding me. We curve to the left just a little that is when somewhere off in the distance I hear the soft lap of water mixed with music. A small smile creeps onto my face as I think about how romantic this is. As we move closer, I believe I recognize what is playing. It sounds like something from the nineteen forties that I had commented about once when we were music surfing on our phones after a long night of hot, sweaty sex. He knows I have a thing for those old crooners.

Gently, Houston directs me to stop. I feel his hand on my arm, no it is his finger actually. He is tracing a line up my forearm as he stands behind me. His assault of my neck tenderly begins. Oh my lord, he knows just how to drive me utterly crazy. Trying to turn around, Houston simply mumbles, "No." His kisses subtly move across my neck. As the sounds from the sensual music takes over my body, I can't stop myself from swaying in time to the music. Tracing my ear with his tongue, he whispers, "Charli, you drive me wild."

His comment spurs me on. Beginning to move even more to the tempo of the music, reaching up I run my hand through his gloriously soft wavy curls. Taking about a half step back, separating our bodies, he says, "Baby, you know I love a good lap dance from you but this is one time I want you to slow down tiger."

I can't help but respond with what I hope is a sexy, "Rarrr."

Still swaying to the music, Houston finally removes my blindfold. It takes my eyes a few minutes to adjust to the remaining light, but when I can really focus what I find before me is a stone and patina aged gazebo jutting into the water. Smiling, I understand that explains the sound of lapping water.

Sighing, I manage to say, "Oh, Houston! It's magnificent."

"I thought you might like it."

"Be careful walking out. There are some small loose stones here and there in the walkway." Walking into the gazebo, I am speechless. The beautiful scene in front of me defies anything I imagined. In the center, is a round wooden table (antique I am sure) set for two with two crystal candlesticks each holding a lit navy candle. (My man and his navy.) Directing us to the table, I notice one wine glass is absent. Reaching into the bag, he withdraws the chest containing my glass. After handing me the glass, he pours each of us a drink. We toast and drink to each other. The music changes to something that is softer without vocals. Dancing to the soothing sounds of a flute, my hands explore his firm muscular chest as I wrap my arms around his neck. With his six foot four frame against my five-six we fit together like a tight fitting glove. Moving gracefully to the music, I realize how at peace with myself I am. I can't remember a time when things have felt this perfect. Lost in the gentle swaying of our bodies, the sound of the lapping water in the background, I have no idea how long we stay this way. What I do know, is it's very difficult for us to break apart.

Kissing the top of my head, he asks, "Charli, are you hungry?"

"Now that you mention it, I am a wee bit hungry."

Raising an eyebrow at me, I can't help but smile sheepishly, "I know, don't say anything, I think the music is influencing me. I'm pretty sure I have never said "wee bit" before in my life."

Smiling, Houston says, "Baby you can say wee bit as much as you like." Pulling me into him, our mouths meet in a tender yet passionate kiss.

Turning, I see sitting on the table two covered dishes. "Wow, either you have some powerful magic to cause food to appear or I was really lost in the music while we were dancing."

Guiding us to the table, he laughs softly saying, "As much as I would like to lay claim to having magic, the food was delivered while I was enjoying holding a very beautiful sexy woman in my arms."

After our meal several people swiftly and silently remove the table and place settings. They replace them with two deep cushioned, white loungers while I stand by feeling awkward. Looking down where the table once stood, I find a navy and gold design in-bedded into the gazebo floor, the pattern is very familiar. I look at it for a moment trying to place where I have seen it. Then, I remember! I look back and forth between Houston and the design a couple of times to be sure. "This is the pattern that is on the floor of your shower, isn't it?"

Smiling, he answers simply "Yes."

As I move to stand in the center of it, my mind is racing. "Why is it the same?"

"I really had planned on us sitting here, enjoying the night and the sounds of the water but now I feel after that meal we should walk. How about you?" As confused as I am, I agree movement would be better than sitting at the moment. "Ok, H. let's walk." Placing my hand in the bend of his arm, he leads us out of the gazebo to a path that skirts the banks of the water.

We walk quite a way enjoying the sounds of the water washing up against the rocks. I am trying my best to remain calm and wait for his answer. The silence between us seems to be evolving into something else. "Houston?"

Chapter 18

As we walk, he begins with a deep breath, "I am sure you have questions as to how I can freely come and go here." Taking another deep breath as if he is preparing to share some hidden secret, I am beginning to get worried. "This estate originally belonged to my great, great grandfather on my Mother's side, Nigel Houston." Stopping for a minute, I look up at him finding a questioning look on that handsome face. Without speaking, I lay my hand onto his muscled chest, tiptoe up and give him a soft kiss. A kiss that I mean to be encouraging. Houston however wants just a little more than encouragement, as he slips his arms around my waist pulling me to him. Our mouths, gently explore each other. Pulling back from him enough to see his eyes, I can't help the smile that spreads across my face.

"That's where your name comes from, then. I assumed it had something to do with the city." Tightening his hold on me, he pulls me to him as I lay my head on his chest. Houston replies, "That's what everyone thinks." With a small laugh he continues on, "When I was in college, I would make up some grand story about being conceived while my parents were visiting Houston, Texas.

I remain wrapped in the warmth of his arms as he explains, "People, especially those of the female kind always thought it was a unique way for my parents to name me. I have to admit, it was a much better story than being named after your great, great grandfather." Nodding my head in agreement, he pulls me closer and runs his hands down my lower back.

Sighing deeply, I share a secret of my own. "It has been my experience, especially when I was younger that some people make jokes and laugh at you when they find out you share your name with a city or a character from a book." Shivering a small bit, I continue, "Kids can be really cruel if they find out something bothers you."

Placing his hands on my behind, keeping me close, he simply says, "I never thought about that. Shall I track them down and require they give you an apology?" Tilting my chin up to look directly into those pools of warm chocolate eyes, he says, "Charli, no one will ever hurt you again if I have any say in it and believe me, Baby, I plan on having a lot of say in your future."

Grinding my hips into him, I respond, "My full name, which I legally changed, is Charlotte Kathryn Jensen and you most certainly will not hunt them down and have them apologize." Attempting to break the seriousness of the moment, I continue with a pat on his chest and ask, " So a lot of say in my future?"

"Yes, quite a lot. But why not Charlotte? What caused you to change your name?"

161

Frowning, I look up into those sensual yet understanding eyes. "I hate the name Charlotte for many reasons but the main one is because of my childhood. I was always teased as a little girl. Kids were forever asking me about my "web."

Taking on a sassy childlike voice, I say, "Charlotte, what ya goanna write in your web? Where does your silk come from? We know where a spider's silk comes from. Do you have spinnerets on your butt, too?" Burrowing my head in his chest for a moment, I add, "it was horrible."

Raising his hand to my face in such a gentle caress, "I am so sorry you went through that when you were younger. Lifting his right hand and saying, "for future reference, I promise I will never ask where your web is or anything about it." Smiling wickedly he does let me know he might ask me where I want to be when I have my next orgasm. Very quickly I let him know that anywhere would be just fine with me.

Taking a step back from him, I look up into those eyes that are alive with desire, "My parents named me after the city they met in, Charlotte, Missouri. I don't know why I just blurted that out to you."

"I have no idea either but I am glad you shared that bit of information with me. For the record, you know how to kill a man's hard on, just talk about your parents." Motioning ahead he says,

"Let's continue our walk, Charli Jensen formerly known as Charlotte Kathryn Jensen. I am thankful your parents met in Charlotte, Missouri."

Stepping in front of me, Houston grasps my shoulders, pulls me into him, and whispers in my ear the last thing I expected in a fake southern accent, "For the record my dear, I must admit I would have changed my name from Charlotte to Charli, too." Carrying on with this playful old southern stuff, I replied in my best belle voice, "Why, Mr. Houston, I do declare. You are just a little scoundrel, aren't you?"

With a slight lift of his brow, he smiles wickedly saying, "Ms. Charlotte if you only knew." Ending our little tribute to the South with great laughter, we continue our walk. I now realize, I have missed this type of thing, having someone to joke and laugh with. Even our laughter seems to complement each other. His deep baritone against my soft singsong laughter, sounds right. It has been awhile since I felt this comfortable to share anything about changing my name. I really didn't mean to tell him but it just came out.

"How do they feel about that?"

Looking just a little confused, I ask, "They who?" but deep in my heart I know who he is referring to.

"Your parents, Charli. How do they feel about you changing your name?"

Stumbling just a little, Houston quickly supports me placing his arm around my waist. "Oh, they don't know." I could feel the old familiar lump in my throat as the topic of my parents came up. Taking a deep breath, I know exactly where this conversation is headed. I don't want to go there not tonight. Blinking back tears, I continue, "They are both deceased. They have been gone a long time. Way before I changed my name." Feeling the lightness of just moments before drifting away I look down at my hands, "I don't want to talk about it or them." Beginning to blink my eyes rapidly, I am determined not to cry. Almost begging Houston, I request, "Please Houston, don't ask."

Somehow, understanding that this wasn't the right time, placing his hands on both sides of my face, gently tilting it up for our eyes to meet, he solemnly answered "I won't. But know I am very sorry. If I could change your loss, I would."

"Thanks" is all I am capable of mumbling as a tear runs down my cheek. Moving his right thumb to wipe it away, he smiles a sorrowful smile as I leaned into his hand. "I'm sorry, Houston, I didn't mean to be short. It's just the anniversary of their deaths is coming soon. This is always a hard time of the year for me. That's one thing about no season changes here in Miami, I am not reminded so much that spring is near. That's when it happened, in the late spring."

Breaking the moment of what he correctly interpreted as my anguish, "You can't help that, it was in your genes" he finished with a fake laugh.

Looking around and down at my legs, I am just a bit confused, "What's in my jeans? I don't have them on?"

Pulling me into him, he laughs and says, "not j-e-a-n-s but g-e-n-e-s. You being short, that is."

"Ha, Ha. Wise ass. Take that," as I swat his chest and childishly stick my tongue out. Focusing the conversation back on this wonderful place, " I must admit, I've wondered how we could come in here after hours so many times without any difficulties. Now, I understand but wait a minute, if your family doesn't own it any more, I still don't get it."

"No one actually owns the estate now. My family is a major contributor to the foundation that maintains it."

Casually nodding, I reply, "So the old saying "money talks" is at work here?"

Barely shaking his head with almost a grimace on his face, Houston replies "Yes, I'm afraid so, Charli."

"I'm not a big fan of the belief, if you got it flaunt it. However, in this case, I suppose flaunting it is allowing you as well as all the visitors here to enjoy Beauty supported with your money."

Sounding serious he says, "Charli, I really don't feel as if I flaunt my wealth but I do use it, my beauty. I do use it. I work very hard for what I have and I am not embarrassed about it."

Realizing, I have upset him, I make a feeble attempt to apologize for what I said but he assures me that things are alright. So I take another stab at it.

Running my hands up his arms, I smile as I continue, "On a personal note, from what I have seen, and I'm pretty sure I've seen it all, you've definitely got it. I like it when you flaunt those muscular abs, those finely sculpted thighs and all your other yummy male parts. I especially like it when you flaunt it when we are alone in your bedroom, on the veranda, in the pool. Do I need to continue?"

"Baby, if you continue I will need to flaunt it right in this very spot."

Continuing on we end our walk, in a moonlight garden which obviously was his plan, I stand taking in the romantic scene in front of me. For most of this night, I've felt as if I were a princess on a stroll with her prince. This is the perfect place to end our stroll. Guiding me to an outdoor sofa in the middle of lush green foliage and orchids, "Shall we sit?" Houston asks. Smiling and nodding yes, I look around to see twinkling candles surrounding us continuing the fairy tale feeling I have experienced all night. Reclining back onto the many cushions lining the back of this massive, outdoor daybed, I sit spellbound as Houston continues with the story of this magnificent place. What I notice as the story continues is the gleam in his eye that almost makes me uneasy. I'm not fearful for myself but fearful for Nigel's tale.

"Nigel disgraced his family by falling in love with his best friend's Mother. That scandal would have destroyed his family, since the McKenna's and the Houston's were not only friends but business partners in multiple successful ventures. Nigel's father chose the family's social status and business over him, sending him to America. Apparently, even back then, business came first and the need for wealth ran in our veins. Upon arriving in this foreign land, he used some of his funds to start a small shipping business. It grew because Nigel had the family's Midas touch. Surprisingly, when his Father died, he also inherited a huge sum of money."

Drawing a breath in, I interrupted Houston. "He inherited money from his Father? Don't you see H. his Father loved him after all? Right? If he wanted to completely eliminate him from his life then he would have taken him out of his will completely."

Looking up into the darkness of the sky commenting, "Baby, I never thought of it that way. I suppose he did love Nigel or he wouldn't have left him anything." Touching Houston on the leg, hopefully encouraging him to continue with his story knowing there has to be more, I inquire, "and?"

He pulls me close, and I lay my head on his shoulder. Seeming lost in the story he says, "Anyway, he used his inheritance to expand his shipping business, GlynisRun, as well as to purchase land. I believe that, I inherited my keen business instincts from dear, old great, great Grandfather Nigel."

Sitting stunned for a moment, processing all the information Houston has just shared with me about this young man and a tale of love gone wrong. Coming to my senses I ask, "Houston, what did you say the shipping business was named?"

Solemnly, he answers, "GlynisRun."

I am sitting here, speechless, staring ahead at a beautiful flower, processing what I've just heard. Holy cow! I knew he's wealthy but not like that. Not GlynisRun wealthy.

"Charli? Are you alright?"

Holding one finger up, I manage to say "Just give me a minute, I'm absorbing this."

With a small laugh, he says "Need some processing time?"

All I can do is nod. After a bit, I finally squeak out, "You have got to be kidding me? GlynisRun is your company?"

"Yes Charli, it is one of them." With a look of confusion, I'm sure, on my face I ask, "Did you say one of them?"

"Yes, one of them. I actually own over fifty companies and stocks in quite a few more." Taking a deep breath as if he is fearful of where this conversation might end, he sheepishly asks, "You've heard of GR, then?"

My head jerks around along with my body turning in one fell swoop. I probably give him my crazy look because all I can say is what I am thinking, "You've got to be kidding? Is there a person around that hasn't see the little red headed boy standing on that hill of green grass yelling at that mysterious someone, Catch, GlynisRun! If you can? I can just see him turning around and running away as he morphs into a man driving off in a delivery van. We get deliveries every week from GR."

I am still trying to process what he has just shared with me as we sit here just enjoying the calm of the night. My head is tilted onto his shoulder, our hands entwined as one, the feel of our bodies touching. Sitting side by side is enough. I have no idea how long we sit this way but he breaks the spell by kissing the top of my head. Houston then breaks our silence by explaining the meal that we shared. "The meal we enjoyed tonight is a traditional Scottish meal accompanied by pan flute music which also was inspired by Scotland as well."

"Hmm."

"When I was planning this little affair, I thought it a fitting tribute to Nigel tonight. Without his misfortune, we wouldn't have this beautiful estate to enjoy."

I have to agree this is a fitting tribute to him. The music was beautiful, H. The meal was delicious. Thank you for sharing Nigel's story with me."

"As the story goes, those goblets we drank out of tonight are from Nigel's and my great, great grandmother's estate. Grandfather Nigel had the pair crafted for Grandmother Penelope once they were engaged. However, he only gave her one, keeping the other for himself. The goblets were to remain separated until the two were united in marriage which would also unite the pair of goblets." I sat there amazed at the romance of this story. "I sent you two hand carved wooden containers." Remembering the mystery behind the second chest and how much it resembled the first, I guess the second had something to do with Nigel, as well.

"How could I forget the second one, it only came today. Let me guess, GR delivered it."

"Of course it did my sexy lady. Who else would I trust with my valuables?"

After pondering this for about thirty seconds, I reply with one of those well duh attitudes, "I see your point. Who else?" Making a silly face, I ask, "Valuables?"

Houston smiles his I know a secret you don't know smile and finally says, "I have no doubt that you would like to know what is in the smaller one."

Smiling and nodding my head, Houston stands and retrieves the chest from the bag. My eyes grow to the size of the full moon overhead as I say, "Let me guess your little elves brought that bag here because I know we didn't."

Smiling that sexy smile of his, he nods saying, "You see, it is beneficial to have an extreme amount of funds. Things happen."

"Ah, don't you mean mega funds, apparently Mr. Donovan?"

Returning to my side, H. gives me a quizzical look. "Really Mr. Donovan?" Clearing his throat, he continues with, "As tech savvy as you are, I assumed you have completed a web search on me, by now and know all about me."

Shaking my head no, I am sure I have just shocked him. "Actually, I don't like to find out about men I may be interested in through some cold and impersonal information on the internet. Call me old school but I like the surprise element."

Nodding his head, looking over at me and stressing the word, "Men? Alright then. I was under the impression, I am keeping you busy enough. If you have time for "men" then perhaps I need to step up my game. As for the might be interested part, let me assure you, if the things we have enjoyed together both sexually and not, are what you do for men you might be interested in, then baby I can't wait to experience our sexual exploits when you are definitely interested."

Quickly smacking the side of his leg, I shoot him my shut up look. Calming down and all joking aside, I notice a certain look of astonishment or deep down maybe it was pride, he nods his head. Taking my hand in his, he squeezes it just enough for me to understand, he likes that. Me not knowing about him and his past. We lounge all the way back on this plush, splendid outdoor sofa, enjoying just being hand in hand. "I like it when you call me H."

"Oh, good because Houston is sooo long," I say in a playful tone. Leaning over and grabbing my waist with his free hand, he finds my spot of weakness.

"I'll teach you to make fun of me." His fingers move across my ribs and I laugh. The more they move the harder I laugh. The harder I laugh, the harder I try to contain the very un-lady like snort my brothers used to tickle me to hear. Holding up my hands and begging, he gives me some mercy and stops. Regaining our composure, I can't help but wonder what his competitors would say if they could see this side of Houston Donovan, world mogul. Sighing as I rest my head on his shoulder, I say softly, "I want to remember this night. I do have to admit something though." I could feel his body tense.

"What is it? I sit up, turn to look at him and realize I've never seen the strange look he has on his face at this moment. "You know, that doesn't mean that Lana didn't check you out and give me some basic info."

"Really? Just what did Lana tell you about me?"

With just a hint of mischievousness in my voice, "I really am not sure your ego can handle what they said."

"Oh, Ms. I know something you don't know, I am pretty sure my ego can handle it."

"Wellllll, she relayed that in her research that a women, no wait maybe is was women anyway, some female said that you were, I believe one quote was- pure liquid gold sex on legs. Having Houston Donovan make love to you was in her imagination what it would feel like to have liquid gold run over your body."

Lifting, his brows just a little, "It did, did it?"

With a slight nod of admission, I continue on. "Yes, but I don't agree."

"Oh you don't? Then perhaps I need to up my game."

"Your game is just fine but if you feel the need to up it, then I am all for that as long as I am the receiver of this improved game." Smiling, I continue. "No, I need to write a response to those that have called you liquid gold sex because they obviously are wrong.   Pulling my hand up to his lips, seductively kissing my palm, "And what would your response be?"

Pretending to be in deep thought, I pause for a minute enjoying the feel of his lips on my palm. I'm not sure I ever knew how sensual kissing my hand could be. Maybe it's not exactly the act that is so sensual but the provider. "I'd respond-not liquid gold but rock solid gold, baby, rock solid gold."

Smirking, he patted the sofa's soft fabric between his legs, "Come over here and sit in front of this, what was it you said-rock solid body."

"Ah, don't let that that little comment about the rock solid stuff go to your head, Mister."

"I really can't help it baby. When a sexy woman like you makes a comment like that about me, I just can't help it going to my head. By the way, it goes to my brain as well."

"Oh my goodness, you are incorrigible."

"Incorrigible or not, I want that pretty little behind right here sitting between my legs feeling what is rock solid."

"That seems to be a thing with you, Mr. Donovan. Me sitting in your lap or in front of you."

Shrugging his shoulders, "You said it was rock solid not me. What the hell, Charli. What is this Mr. Donovan crap? Are we back to that then, Ms. Jensen?" Asking with some contempt in his voice.

"Calm down, H." I respond as I roll my eyes. "Oh Lord, it's not like I said anything you don't already know, you are rock solid thanks to those hours you spend in your gym at all those random times of the day and night. What do you mean, are we back to that? You are Mr. Donovan" shrugging my shoulders, "Sometimes, I just like to say it."

With a calm quickly returning to his face, "Since that's settled, now back to the matter at hand, can you think of a better place for you to sit than right here in front of me?" Patting the seat one more time and saying in his best creepy voice, "The better to kiss your neck my dear."

Looking from side to side around us, "You've talked me into it but I just want to ask you two things."

"Alright, what is it? Ask away."

"First, are any of your little elves going to magically appear?"

Making his eyes big in an exaggerated way, and shaking his head, "I didn't know you were into that sort of thing but I suppose…"

"Houston Donovan, you know better than that!" as I smack his leg.

"Well, if you say so. Darn it! As for elves, I don't have any but I do have something that is magically delicious or so I have been told."

"If you don't stop teasing me, I am going to get up, go stand over by that bush and leave you sitting here alone. I do agree you are magically delicious but what is the point if there is no one to enjoy all the yumminess."

"Oh really, alone, huh?" Pausing for just a second, "No Baby, they are gone. This section of the estate has been closed for the night and no one, including the security will dare to come near us."

"As for the second thing, I wanted to ask you, you sounded like the big bad wolf, when you were talking about kissing my neck. So does that mean, you are going to devour me?"

"Come on over here and find out." Smiling, he moves his legs apart, and pulls me across his lap guiding me to sit down. Then he wraps his strong arms around me as if I am inside a cocoon. When we are like this, laughing and joking, I really do forget that the man with me is a cutthroat businessman that has thousands of people in his employ and hundreds at his beck and call twenty-four hours a day.

I lean back against Houston's firm chest as he whispers into my ear, "Charli, during these past six months since you came into my life, my views on a great many things have changed. I have no idea where my future will take me. What I do know, I want you to go with me. I am not sure that I believe in the institution of marriage but I do believe in the way you make me feel."

I swallow deeply, really at a loss for words. My heart is racing faster than any car ever dared to go. I sit here trying to interpret what is happening. I answer with a bit of confusion. I know he can hear the perplexity in my shaky voice as I speak. "I feel the same way, Houston." Lifting an antique key from somewhere beside us, he holds both the key/chest out in front of us. (I know he can feel the deep breath I take.) Houston unlocks, what I have come to refer to as my little chest, placing it in my hands.

"Open it, Baby."

Following his simple directions, I lift the lid of this intricately carved box, slowly exhaling the breath that I didn't realize I have been holding. Laying on a bed of black velvet is an antique emerald and diamond heart shaped necklace. It is the most stunning piece of jewelry, I think I have ever seen. Supporting my trembling hands from underneath Houston calmly says into my ear, "This necklace represents a great many things to me Charli. It has been in my family for a number of years. Nigel gave this piece to Penelope when they were first betrothed."

I sit staring with my mouth open. I am completely stunned at this gleaming beauty. If anyone dared to approach us, they would have almost physically felt the love radiating from us. Even though, neither has ever used that four letter word, I know in this moment as I sat staring at this heart that I love this man. Suddenly, understanding the significance of this night, all the family heritage pieces; Houston Donovan has put this night together for me because vintage pieces and history are so important to me. This is my special night. A night that

I will someday tell my daughters about. The night that was made just for me.

I look over my shoulder as a lone tear slips down my check. The only person I can't tell is the one that would have been the happiest for me, my Mother. "Houston, will you please put this exquisite necklace on me?"

Gently wiping my tear he leans around and looks at me with a question in his eyes, "Are you sure?"

"Yes, H. I am more than sure. I know deep in my soul that I want you to."

"When, I close the clasp on this piece of jewelry, we are closing the doors of our lives to others. Do you understand that?" Smiling so big, there could be no doubt, I lift the box to him.

"Charli, I also want you to think about moving into the penthouse with me. Let's see where this is going."

"Ahh, I'm not too sure about that Houston."

"We'll discuss that later, I think the time of talking is over." We lay there in each other's arms celebrating the commitment each has just made to the other.

Chapter 19

My phone is ringing. I look at the number, roll my eyes and take a deep breath. "Hello."

"Hey, sis. How are you?"

"I'm fine and you?"

"I'm good."

"What have you been up to lately, Charli?"

"Just working. As a matter of fact, I am sitting at my desk at this very moment. Why?"

"No reason."

"What about you John?"

"Same here, work, then home."

"I did have something interesting happen to me the other day."

Ah, here is the actual reason for this call. "Oh, really, what was it?" I silently exhale.

"I ran into the Speedy Grab, for a loaf of bread, there I am standing in the checkout waiting for the little lady in front of me to pay for her dog food and toilet paper. I look over at those magazines they have for all the teenage girls and the Hollywood lovers, can you guess what I saw?"

I wince because I know where he is heading. Speaking of teenagers, I suppose, I need to utilize the skill that I developed as a teenager myself. I believe my parents called it lying. I always preferred to refer to it as stretching the truth.

"Charli, are you there?"

"Sorry, John. I got lost in the visual. I've no idea what you saw?"

"A picture of my baby sis in a bathing suit that was barely covering up her woman parts, walking down the beach holding some mega-zillionaire's hand."

"Woman parts? Mega-zillionaire? Really? You have got to be kidding me?"

"The magazine called him that. Yes, woman parts, you're my sister. That's what you have, woman parts. I can't call them anything else. Can you imagine how I felt, trying to buy bread when I saw that?"

"No, I have no idea how you felt. I can only try to imagine."

"What the hell were you thinking, Charli?"

"Oh! My! Gosh! I was on the beach what's the big deal? Besides you're my brother not my keeper."

"How would they have felt?"

"I don't know. If they were alive, I wouldn't be here. Don't John. Just don't play the Mom and Dad card."

"Well, it was a little embarrassing but it irritated me, not irritated but… it pissed me off to find out you are involved with someone from the front of some gossip magazine."

"John, I'm not sure what Houston and I are, right now. We have been seeing a lot of each other but I don't know, so let's see. How weird would it be to call you up and say-Hey Bro, I just wanted you to know, I've meet this great guy, who is filthy dog rich. We have great sex. His...

"Woe! That is enough of that. I know you have sex, at least I assume you do, you are my little sister so let's just leave it at that. I really don't need a visual as you say. Damn, Charli now I have to erase that from my head."

"Well, welcome to my world. It took me years and years to erase the images I had from you and Brad and the things I heard. Really, John, one little picture? Point for little sis. Who says I don't know how to work my brother.

"Listen Sis, you deserve this. It's nice to think that you are having some fun, again. Lord knows you haven't had any fun in a really long time."

"Thanks. It feels pretty nice."

"Now, just do me a favor and buy a one piece bathing suit."

Laughing, I reply, "I'll think about it." Catching up for just a little longer, I fill him in on how our business is growing. He tells me how he is playing basketball in a league. After about fifteen minutes of catching up, we say our goodbyes promising to not let so long go between our next call. I also made him promise two things, to talk to our other brother, Bradley, about the picture and to stop looking at those trash magazines.

The time is quickly approaching for the Black and Gold Gala. After a brief but intense discussion, we decided to go. I definitely have my reservations but I do believe this is event will be good for our business. Lana and I head out for a day of shopping. Every time I go out to any store that might possibly carry a dress for the gala, I look. I've been doing this since Lana and I agreed that the gala might be the very thing to push Supreme Corporate Travel into the limelight. I have designated today as the day. It's the day I'm bringing home a dress to wear if it kills me. I am meeting Lana and Rose at The Java House, we are going to spend some time catching up and the three of us are heading out for a day of shopping in some vintage stores.

What are you doing, beautiful?
Shopping. U?
Meetings all day
Yuck, on Saturday!
Afraid, so. Pictures from the dressing room????
Maybe... Possibly... More than likely... Ok. Next one ;) ;) ;)
That's my girl
When will you be back?
Couple of days.

"I can't believe I found the dress, it even looks great with my necklace," I say to Lana as I enter into my building's parking area.

"OH MY GOD!" Charli, what in the world is going on?"

"I have been with you all day, remember? How would I know? Probably some nut job has gone off the deep end. Just my luck they would live in my complex." As I put the car into park, I get just a little scared when I hear people yelling, that's her car! There she is! Have you seen Houston today? The next thing I know, a crowd is moving toward us. "Lana, what am I supposed to do?"

"I don't know but I can tell you what you shouldn't do and that's get out of this car."

Just as I am trying to back out of the space two police cars arrive. They get the crowd under control and most of them leave. Apparently, they just wanted my picture. The officers advise me to find another place to spend the night which will help calm everything down if I am at an undisclosed location. They assure me that this kind of thing happens in Miami quite often. They also tell me more than likely it will be blown over by tomorrow or just as soon as some scandal breaks over in South Beach.

I am spending the night at Lana's. On the way to her place out in Coral Way, we decide a girl's night is much needed. We text Rose and Joan, they are calling a couple of our other friends. So the six of us will be doing the comedy movie thing, mixing margaritas and laughing till our sides hurt. Just what I need. We are about half way through the first movie, the second round of drinks was beginning to fill our glasses, when Lana's doorbell rings. We all look at each other, my heart begins to pound. Lana walks over to the door, peeks out the peephole, turns and smiles. Opening the door wide, standing there is Terrance with a couple of friends. What turned into a girl's night has now turned into a party. Well, since I'm staying here tonight, you know that old saying, if you can't beat'em, join'em.

Chapter 20

It is good to just sit around, talking and laughing. Not having to worry about impressing anyone, not having to worry if my makeup is just right, not having to worry about the way I am dressed, is it just sexy enough but not over the top. Yep, it is good. Everyone is just having a good time. Music, laughter, food, conversation. I almost feel like I have time traveled back to our apartment at the University, when this was the only way we could afford to unwind.

"Charli, that's some necklace you have on."

Reaching up, I touch the special piece lovingly. "Thanks, Terrance."

"Terry, please."

"OK, Terry."

"Someone special?"

As I smile, I pick up the heart shaped necklace, and nod, "yes, someone very special."

"Good for you! You know, I've noticed when you come in JH, you seem happier." Nodding his head toward my neck he asks, "Is he, I'm assuming it is he, the reason?" Shaking his head, "Wait a minute, does any of that make sense?"

Laughing just a little, "Yes, it all makes sense. Let's see if I can answer your questions. Yes, he is a he and yes he is the reason I am happier."

Giving me a one arm hug, he turns and walks away. No wonder Lana likes him, he seems to be really good for her. As we are winding down this impromptu party, taxis are called. Everyone heads out with the exception of me and Terry. I say my goodnights to Lana and Terry, I am not sure they really heard me, as I slip into my room for the night. Just about the time my head hits the pillow, I remember my phone.

"Crap!" I am really too tired to get up and check on it. Oh yeah, it was dead earlier when I put it on the charger. It should be charging. I roll over and drift to sleep.

Sometime the next morning, I faintly hear Terry leaving. Lying in bed, I am just beginning to wake up, when Lana knocks on the door. "Charli, are you awake?"

Moaning, "Sort of, why? Let me guess, you want to come in here and tell me how many, Oh Terry's! You said last night? Oh wait, it was probably too many to count or you lost count at some unbelievable number. Well, I could really give you some numbers but I always lose count with my chocolate haired sex machine. So just take that!" Pulling the pillow over my head, I simply want her to go away and let me sleep. After all, it is the weekend.

"Funny, smart ass but you better get up and get out here."

"Why? Is the sky falling, little chicken?"

"It's not falling and you mean Chicken Little goof ball not little chicken. You've got to see this."

"See what?" I ask as I drag myself out of bed and into her living room. All I can do is stand there wide eyed. Finally, I manage a "What the hell? Forgive me Mama but really what the freakin hell?" Walking over to the window, all I see out front is all types and sizes of people with cameras. "Oh Shit, Lana!"

"Oh shit is right girl. My neighbors are going to freak out."

Lana, do you think they are here for me?"

"Well, let's see Charli, I have lived here almost two years and while last night with Terry was fantastic, I really don't think they are here because of my epic "Oh Terry's," she replies smacking my arm.

"Lana, what am I supposed to do?"

"I don't know. Call your man. That's what I would do."

"I really don't want to do that but you're right he will know."

Jerking up the phone, I text Houston.
Shit Storm at Lana's. Call ASAP.

No response. "He must be in a meeting."

Lana looks at me with her hands on her hips. "Seriously? A meeting on Sunday?"

Raising my shoulders in a slow shrug, I answer sort of shakily, "Well, I don't know but I do know he would answer me if he could." Thinking for a moment I asked, "Lana, did you call the police?"

"Sure Charli, didn't you hear me? Hello officer, there are about fifty people standing on the sidewalk in front of my house with cameras." Shaking her head for effect, "No officer, they aren't attacking me. No officer, they aren't rushing my property." She looks at me and slowly nods for emphasis. "Yes officer, they are standing on the sidewalk peacefully right now." Smacking my shoulder and asking me in her well duh voice, "What do you think the police are going to do? Cause, last time I heard – It's still a free country and they aren't doing anything wrong."

A couple of hours drag by with still no response from Houston. I check my phone several times willing it to make some type of noise, especially Houston's ring. No matter how much I try to forget those people out front, I just can't. I go to the door, open it and look out. The cameras go crazy. People start yelling. I quickly close the door. Looking at Lana I ask, "Do you think it's been a slow celebrity day on South Beach?" We look at each other and laugh, even though my head hurts like ten grizzly bears are having a dance party up there. Finally, deciding to take advantage of me being here we work or at least pretend to work. Thank goodness, I saved my latest projects to the cloud. I use Lana's desktop while she is on her laptop. I am having a difficult time concentrating but I don't want my faithful friend to know. Lana picks up my phone as it goes off. Somehow she knew, I just don't want to deal with it.

"Charli, who is Jeffery? Do you know a Jeffery? Cause his name just came up on the screen." "Geez, inquisition or what? Yes, I know him. He is one of Houston's drivers." She tries to hand me my phone. Holding my hand up and shaking my head no, "Just read it to me. It's not like it is going to be top secret."

Sighing, Lana puffs just a little,
Stay inside, Mam. On my way.

"Well, wasn't that just helpful? Like I am going to let you go running out into a street filled with whoever/whatever you call them, paparazzi, I suppose." We stop and look at each other as if we have just had a giant revelation.

"Lana, how in the world did we miss this?"

"I have absolutely no idea. Oh my goodness, Charli. You have the paparazzi after you."

Mam, I'm coming to the door. They won't move off the sidewalk. You're fine.

I stand beside the door, jerk it open. Jeffrey enters Lana's, what used to look spacious, foyer. Now it is filled with this walking, talking hulk. Ever the man on the job, looking me up and down he asks, "Mam, are you ok? Are you both ok?"

"Yes, Jeffery we are both fine. Thank you for coming."

Nodding his head, "My pleasure, Ma'am."

"Jeffery, come into the kitchen. I'm going to get a glass of water. Do you want a drink of something?"

Following me into Lana's kitchen in the back of the house, "Thank you, Ma'am but no I am fine." Holding up his hand Jeffery continues all business, "Ma'am, we have a three step plan of action."

Pointer finger goes up. "One. Get you out of here and to the penthouse."

Second finger up "Two. Get your car away from Ms. Lewis' home. May I suggest, next time park in the garage.

Third finger up "Three. Retrieve any items you may need from your apartment."

With a brief pause, which I can only assume is for effect, Jeffery continues on. "Steps one and three will go off simultaneously with a forty-five minute delay before step two occurs."

We just stand for a moment while I stall by drinking my water. It feels almost like he is waiting for my go ahead. I suppose that is what happens with Houston. Jeffrey presents the course of action, Houston approves or disapproves. Who am I to keep what sounds like a good plan from happening? With a curt nod, I respond, "Sounds as if you have it all worked out, I suppose I am ready to leave whenever you think is best. I do believe sooner rather than later is best for Lana. Especially since she is worried about how her neighbors might be feeling about all of this."

Jeffrey nodded his appreciation for my acknowledgement but I think his plan was happening with or without my approval. Somehow, I think Houston has already approved it. Walking out to Lana, he explains, "We will be leaving in just a few minutes. Ms. Jensen has expressed your concern about your neighbors. I don't know this neighborhood but from the looks of the well-kept lawns and homes, I would say most of your neighbors are secretly enjoying this. They may complain for a few days but they also have something to tell their families/friends about. Right now, most of them are probably wondering who is in the house and why all those cameras are out there. Now if you'll excuse me, I need to make a few calls. If it is alright with you I will just step out back to your screened in porch to make them."

I look at Lana. "Well, I am not sure what to say about all of this other than it has been an interesting twenty-four hours."

Laughing, she hugs me and agrees. "Will you be in the office tomorrow?"

"Lana, at this point I could be in Tim Buk To tomorrow. Who knows? I promise I'll let you know." Jeffery re-enters the kitchen, nods toward Lana, "Ma'am, it was nice meeting you. I believe everything will calm down once Ms. Jensen leaves the area."

"Oh. Ok. You know she is safe here. You really didn't need to come and get her."

With no emotion at all, Jeffery looks at Lana saying, "Ma'am, Mr. Donovan instructed me to pick Ms. Jensen up from this address and safely ensconce her into his Miami Penthouse, Dade 303." Sounding like Houston's words were law, Jeffery turns, looks at me as if to say-time to go, Ma'am and heads toward the door.

I know what is coming if I know Lana at all. I look over at her just about the time she opens her mouth and before I can intervene she blurts out, "Well, if Mr. Donovan said so by all means it must happen immediately."

"Lana, he is right and so is Houston. I would hate for anything to happen to you or your home because I am too stubborn to go with him." Crossing the room, I give her a hug and whisper in her ear, "Besides, I can't take two nights of Oh Terry! I'm coming! I'm coming!"

Just before we step out, Jeffery instructs me on what will probably happen. How I should continue to walk toward the SUV, look forward and not speak. Looking at me, he places his large hand on my arm for support, "Ma'am, I am here to ensure your safety. No one will get to you or harm you. I will read the situation and if I feel it necessary, I will pull you into the security of my body wrapping my arm around you. You also need to brace yourself for anything that might be said. These people can be very cruel. They will say or do just about anything to get a response. It will probably be ugly. Do you understand?"

I am sure my eyes got really big while he was talking. "Yes, Jeffery, I understand. "Oh and Jeffery,"

"Yes, Ma'am?"

"I do feel safe with you because I know Houston trusts you."

Smiling he replies, "You are right, Mr. Donovan trusts me, Ma'am."

Saying something into his Bluetooth, he looks at me, and gives me a nod. I nod back. The next thing I hear, "It's a go. I repeat, it's a go."

Jeffrey opens the door. We walk out. People begin yelling my name. Cameras start popping all around me. I hear, "Do you and your associates have these type of partner sharing gatherings often?"

"How long have you and Houston Donovan been together?"

"Does he like a good threesome?"

"Is this a love nest for you and your business partner?"

"Has your secret lesbian affair dated back to the time you were college roommates?"

All of these questions are about to make me sick. I want to stop and set the record straight but I felt Jeffery tighten up on my arm. I know I heard him mumble "Keep walking." Just as we reach the end of Lana's drive, a very familiar navy blue SUV rolls to a stop. I have never been so happy to see a vehicle in all my life. The back door opens, Jeffery helps me in, he climbs in beside me. We speed away. They handle this as if this is an everyday thing for them. Is this what Houston goes through? I sit in stunned silence. I thought those people were harmless when I was in the safety of Lana's house. There are sick, vile creatures yelling those horrible things at me. I lean back and sit with my eyes closed until I feel us enter the underground garage at Dade 303.

Chapter 21

My eyes remain closed as I sit in the seat, trying to collect myself. It doesn't matter how tightly I squeeze to keep them shut, the vision of those people, pushing toward me is burned into my head. The questions hurled at me were vile. Never, even after the accident, have I been ask anything as repulsive as what they yelled at me. Trying to get my mind to focus on something more pleasant, I think back to the night Houston and I were setting on this very seat. We were heading back to the city after a day down on the keys. The things his wandering hands did to me. I can't stop myself from smiling. (I'm not too sure but there is a possibility a little moan escaped my lips.) Touching my face, it feels a little flushed. The way his hand caressed my inner thigh. The tingling sensation I had as he leaned across the seat unbuckled my belt and moved me into his lap. Thank god, it was dark. I can still hear him whisper, "Baby, I like you fastened on top of me."

Remembering, I'm not alone and that I am actually sitting in the downstairs garage, I know I must focus on today. Houston is off somewhere on his quest for world domination. Actually, I think he is in Dallas. What I am sure of is that Jeffery is sitting beside me not H. I readjust myself in the seat, bringing me back to the day's reality. The driver is still behind the wheel, also. Are they waiting for direction from me? Well, we are all in serious trouble then, because I have no clue as to what to do. Keeping my eyes closed, I'm attempting to focus on this moment, and I finally speak.

"Jeffery."

"Yes, Ma'am."

"Thank you for rescuing me today."

"Your welcome, Ma'am. Anytime. Opening my eyes, looking across at one of Houston's other cars I really just want this horrible experience to end. With a feeble smile I see in the window's reflection, I draw a deep breath, then glance toward the elevator. "I suppose I should stay here for the rest of the day." With a nod of agreement, and an "OK, Kirk" operation remove Charli from the SUV commences. Exiting the SUV, Kirk opens the door for me. I hope the next thing I hear is something about being beamed up to the penthouse, since Kirk was driving the vehicle. This day has just been that strange. So much for my secret longing of being teleported to a far-away land where the paparazzi doesn't exist. My childhood of television reruns is coming back to haunt me. Once again, I have my brothers to thank.

I'm looking out the window at the right minute, I suppose, looking but not actually seeing much as Kirk bends over to pick up an object lying on the ground when I see his gun. I assume it's a Glock. At least, that is what the weapon of choice seems to be in the movies. As he rises, I glance up at his face and smile. Remembering back to the days with my brothers, if a man didn't want you to know he was "packing heat" (Hello, Midwest girl.) then you keep your mouth shut. Kirk is wearing a jacket so, keeping my mouth shut is the right choice, I suppose. I know any comment I can possibly make about his gun will do one of two things. First option, make me sound like an idiot. Second option, make me sound naive and feel like an idiot. Neither option is good for me, so I simply make my brothers proud and keep my mouth shut. It's not as if a gun makes me uncomfortable, I grew up around them. I just never thought about Houston's men carrying them. Looking over at Jeffrey, I wonder if he has one and where it is. As if I can't make it upstairs by myself, which truthfully I probably can't, they both escort me to the elevator. Jeffrey inserts his key card, the door opens, with the three of us stepping inside. Again, he inserts his card and away the three of us go. This really surprises me because I have never seen any of Houston's other men upstairs.

Entering the penthouse makes me feel safe. I walk over to the wall of glass, to enjoy the scene below. As far as penthouses go, this one isn't very high, twentieth floor, but the view from all sides is spectacular. This building is very exclusive. I have no doubt that the paparazzi will not break the building's boundaries. Even if they do, the building security will handle them swiftly, of that I am sure. I stand here in this room alone. Jeffery and Kirk have disappeared into some room within this vast space. Probably to Nash's office, which I really have no idea which of the many rooms that is. I think it is one of the two rooms that connect with Houston's. Undoubtedly, if I make any type of sound out of the ordinary, one or both of them will be to my rescue within seconds.

Just as Jeffery, who seems to be everywhere, enters the room, the elevator arrives allowing a man and a woman to step into the glass foyer. I notice they have my things. Forcing a smile as they enter, I walk across the space that separates us. Jeffery and the man exchange a brief nod. He simply says, "Upstairs, Mr. Donovan's room." Without any type of response, they leave us alone.

Returning to the wall, I contemplate going out onto the veranda. Even though I have been in Miami almost a year this blasted heat still does me in which forces me to rethink the veranda idea. This day has finally gotten to me. I rub my left shoulder while I stand here, beginning to question if Houston is worth this. As silent tears slip down my cheeks, I berate myself for entertaining such a foolish notion. Of course, he is worth this. Turning from a view that would normally calm the storm that remains inside me, I look at my rescuer, "Jeffrey, I can't talk to Houston, can I?"

Shaking his head, "No Mam. I am afraid not." Giving him my best, pretty please smile that always worked on my older brother I get nowhere. Exhaling a deep breath, "Ok. I already knew that I suppose. He would have called if he was available. I'm sure."

"Yes, Ma'am, I am sure he would."

He stands looking at me with a solemn face. My voice trembling a bit I ask, "Can you at least tell me where he is or when I might hear from him? I just want to hear his voice."

He shakes his head, "Ma'am, I can't answer your questions I am very sorry." With a deep breath, I turn and walk up the steps. This is the first time in our relationship that Houston has been unreachable. It really sucks! I suppose this is what happens when you are involved with a GA zillionaire. I want him to know just how much I need him, so I pick up my phone.

I'm lonely! Where are you? When will you be back? I need your arms around me. It's been too long. ☹

I press send. There, I hope that makes you feel as bad as I do right now.

I want to take a shower to wash the day away but instead I walk into the closet. My eyes are drawn to the array of multi-colored sea-island cotton dress shirts. I run my hand across each of them as I walk down the neatly hung row. Stopping at my favorite, the white/blue stripe poplin. If I can't have him, I'll have to settle for the next best thing as I take it off the hanger. Next, I walk to his vanity, open a drawer, pull out a bottle and spray some of the contents onto the shirt. Burying my face in it, I close my eyes and inhale deeply. It smells like Houston. Quickly, pulling off my clothes and tossing them into the laundry, I put his shirt on and head back into the bedroom.

Sitting down on Houston's side of the bed, I press the remote. The gentle sounds of Old Blue Eyes begin to play. My thoughts flash back to the last time we made love to this track. Sighing deeply, my body begins to heat thinking about that morning he was leaving. I was dressed, ready to walk out the door but for some reason I couldn't. H was in bed, watching me dart around the room trying to get myself together using any excuse to stay. We both understood that I was putting off having to kiss him goodbye. We were talking. This track was playing on the surround sound because he knows how it helps me remain calm. Walking by the end of the bed, suddenly my inner sex kitten came out. Stopping, I turned to face him. I pulled what little of the sheet was over him, off. Standing at the end of this bed admiring the full-length view of his powerful body, committing to my memory every inch of the way he looked at that moment. I began to unbutton my blouse giving him a slow, sensual striptease that almost makes me blush. Crawling onto the bed, I kissed my way up every toned muscular inch of my man. Needing a release to the desire we were feeling, I slowly joined our heated bodies together. As one, we rode the wave of passion to a sweet surrender. Houston didn't leave on time that morning and I was very late to work. Pulling the cover back, I know with that memory in my head I can lie down on his pillow, wrap myself in the comforter and feel safe. I feel as close to him as I can without him being here.

The darkness is everywhere. I'm moving but I'm not walking. I'm on some type of bed, I think. "Where am I?" I scream. I'm not by myself. I hear people talking. "I can't see. I can't see." I try to raise my head but I can't. I can't move my hands or my feet. I jerk. Sitting about halfway up, blinking my eyes I look around. Plop, I'm on my back, staring at the ceiling. I realize I'm still on Houston's side of the bed, which puts a smile on my face like very few things can. I like it here. See, you can move I say to myself as I lift my hands. I lay very still listening. No, I don't hear any voices. The track has ended. I suppose, I forgot repeat. Oh, well. With a small half smile, I realize, I was dreaming. It was just a different version of the same old nightmare. I would have preferred for it to be a Houston centered dream but I suppose I'll have to settle for his side of the bed and my memories of that morning that I can stir up.

I didn't mean to fall asleep, I should have known better than to lie down listening to the crooner. I swear either this comforter or this bed has some type of sleep inducing powers. (Unless Houston's in bed with me. Then sleep on this bed is just about the last thing on my mind.) It is so soft and fluffy. Every time, I lay down my eyes seem to close automatically. Then, I just drift off to sleep. If H. is here with me in this pleasure place of his, then I am generally on cloud nine. Closing my eyes, I create an image of Houston in my head, which makes me smile. Turning my head, "um" I inhale almost rubbing my nose into his pillow. "It still smells a little like Houston," I say to an empty room.

"What smells like me?"

My eyes fly open, did I imagine hearing his voice. I rub my eyes in case I am dreaming. No, I'm awake. I turn my head in the direction of where I thought I heard him. Leaning against the frame of the closet door on the far side of the room in all his irresistible glory, is Houston. Standing just a few feet away is the sexiest man alive. Suddenly, all the obnoxious and hurtful words hurled at me today fade into nothingness. His jacket off, he walks toward me loosening his tie and pulling the wrinkled shirt out of his pants.

I manage to untangle myself from what just mere moments ago was a sleep induced Houston cocoon. My hands are craving to touch him, to feel him, to have more than a memory, to actually have him inside me. I fling myself toward him wrapping my arms around his neck and my legs around his waist. Immediately burying my face into his neck,

I'm feeding all my senses with the real thing. I manage to mumble, "You're back!"

It would appear so." With a sexy, slow smile he continues, "I gather from this greeting you missed me." Sliding down to the floor, I can feel his lean muscles, along with his delicious hard erection. Smacking his chest, "You know I missed you."

"If you slither down me like that each time I am away, then expect me to be away quite a bit." Holding up one finger he says, "Let me think. I believe I received a text from a woman babbling on something about needing my arms. From what I just felt, it is quite possible that you might need more than my arms."

Smiling, I add, "You, sir know I need much more than your arms." Reaching out to touch what I know to be an erection, my smile grows as does Houston. He stutters a little but quickly recovers and continues, "As I was saying before I was felt up, maybe it wasn't you that sent the text. No, I'm certain it came from a number that identified you as the sender. Wait, maybe I should be more careful about who I discuss my texts with." The mischievous smile that is dancing across his face, only adds fuel to the fire burning within my body.

Loving this, playful mood. I join in the teasing. Trying my best to give him a serious look, "You know, I'm not sure if I did or not." With a crooked half smile, he continues, "It sounds like you are having issues, let me read the text in question to refresh your memory." Reaching into his pants pocket, producing his phone he reads, "*I'm lonely! Where are you? When will you be back? I need your arms around me. It's been too long. ☺.*"

"I missed you. I hope you know that. What I really missed is…" reaching for the buttons on his shirt my hands are itching to get him out of his clothes. Taking a small step back, lifting his eyebrows just a little as he asks, "What are you doing?"

Smiling a seductive, take me smile, I answer, "Unbuttoning you, stranger."

Raising his voice just enough for me to pause, he says "Stranger? Don't tell me I have been gone so long you have forgotten my name. Do you need to be reminded of how I feel as I drive myself deep into you? The things I do to your body?"

I pause my hands midair. With a questioning look, I stand there for just a second trying to process what he is saying when he puts my hands down at my sides. In a voice, I know is Houston's but in a tone, I've never heard before he simply says, "Lie down, and don't move." Not understanding why he is talking this way but finding myself eager to follow directions, I lie down. It's almost as if he has some hypnotic, power radiating from those brooding, brown eyes.

Finally, he puts his hands under my knees and pulls me to him. With hands lingering, I feel subtle caresses on the tender skin behind my knees. With each circular motion his hands move up, stopping on my outer thighs. Grasping the hem of my/his shirt, he taps my hip, saying "raise up." He pulls it up to my waist. Next comes, "sit up." Once I am sitting, he slowly teasingly pulls the shirt raising my arms above my head as he goes. "Lie down Baby, keep your arms above your head and let me look at you. I love your body, Charli. Not too thin. Perfect. I hate those thin women that look as if they are a bag of bones. I like curves, you truly are perfect. Your curves give me something to look at; something I can get my hands onto. You curve in all the right places, Baby."

Crawling onto the bed, straddling my legs, he moves the shirt up to my wrists. Gathering it together, holding it in one hand it becomes cloth handcuffs. Because of his position over me, all I can barely do is raise my head

"Head down, close your eyes and keep them closed. I'll stop if you open them. Do you want me to stop baby?"

With a ragged breath, I manage to moan, "No."

"What do you want, Charli?"

"You."

"You are mistaken my sweet, I didn't ask who you want, I ask what you want. Now, can you answer me correctly?" I nod my head because I'm afraid I might say the wrong thing.

"Do I need to ask the question again to refresh your memory because I have a feeling based upon the way your body is trying to move against me that the question isn't what my woman is focusing on at this minute?"

Nodding again, with a smile on my face, I hear the question, "What do you want, Charli?"

"I want you to make me forget today."

I feel light kisses just below my right breast. My ragged breathing lets him know all he needs to. Slowly licking my lips, I crave more. The tip of his tongue continues the assault across my body, barely touching my skin. Moving upward nipping playfully into my swollen breast, the fire inside me is quickly growing to an inferno.

"I missed you my sweet." Moaning with desire that I can no longer contain, he either kisses or licks my tingling skin between each word. He knows exactly what he is doing to me, driving me crazy with desire.

"Do you remember the text, now? Is a my arms around you all you need or did you just say you want me?"

"Houston," is all I can moan.

Continuing the slow torture of his tantalizing touch, he begins switching between his tongue, the tip of his nose and kisses as he continues his maddening journey upward. Holding my arms above my head, he is cutting off all my sense of touch. Damn him, he knows exactly what he is doing.

"Even waking from sleep, you smell alluring, Charli."

Inhaling deeply, "I missed your smell, too," he mumbled into my neck. "Gathering my thoughts I managed to say, "I want to touch you." You aren't playing fair by using my shirt against me.

"I beg your pardon my sweet temptress, it is my shirt and I will use it any damn way I choose." With my increasing desire to feel any part of him against me, I turn to him. He finally takes my lips plunging his tongue into my mouth.

"OH MY GOD!"

Mumbling in the deepest, sexiest voice I think I have heard, "No baby, I'm Houston not God," as he smirks.

"What have you been drinking?"

"Why my dear Charli, I've been indulging in good ole sour mash whiskey from the bluegrass state of Kentucky."

The passion with which he took my lips just seconds ago felt wonderful but the smell that escapes him eliminates my desire. How did I not smell this when I literally jumped into his arms?

"You smell like a brewery."

He quickly releases the shirt that is restraining my hands and he rolls off me. I pull it down as I sit up turning to look at him putting my bent leg up onto the bed.

"I had a few on the plane and possibly a few since I've been home."

My eyes grew wide, "Since you've been home? How long have you been here?"

He hesitates before he answers, his facial expression changing from passion to what seems like anger in a matter of seconds, "I don't know but before you."

The tone wounds me but the words break my heart.

"How could you have been here when I came in? Let me understand this, while I laid in your bed, on your pillow, needing your arms around me, YOU were in this penthouse somewhere? Were you sitting inside your locked office that has all of your truly personal items? You know the things you don't want me to see. Were you doing that while I wandered around this quiet mausoleum? I needed you to tell me everything would be fine! I needed to feel your kiss and to hear you call me Baby!"

Standing up, he turns around. When I looked at him, our eyes locked. "Well, Baby! It's not always about you and what your needs are."

Realizing, I need space and that at this very moment I need to get away from him, I walk out of the room, down the stairs and into the elevator. I push the button and wait for it to stop. I get out and just stand. Now what?

Chapter 22

I really don't know why I came up to the pool. That's not actually true. I do know why because my other option when I was in the elevator was to go to the ground floor. Wouldn't that make for delicious headlines for all those tabloids? Me storming into the lobby in Houston's shirt, hair mussed and no shoes. Of course, the shirt I have on is longer on me than some of my dresses. Grimacing at the thought, I am grateful that I did have enough sense to push the up button. This gets me far enough away but not too far. I have no idea how long I've been standing here.

Suddenly, I realize I'm being a selfish bitch. So what if he smells like a vat of whiskey. He came home to me. He could have ignored the text or simply text back. Who the hell am I to question him like that? We're not married. We don't even live together. What I do know is he is special, very special.

Walking over to the elevator, I can't get down to him fast enough. Stepping into the glass foyer that I thought was so clever when I first came here, I realize just how much he means to me. For the second time in my life, I am deeply in love. Smiling, I begin searching for my magnificent man, at least I hope he is still mine. I have some serious apologizing to do. I know just how I want to apologize. More than likely he is in his office. Turning the knob, I get a surprise. The door is locked. I eliminate all his downstairs hangouts, before moving up a level. I'm beginning to get a little nervous. What if he left while I was in full-blown bitch mode? Do I go home and possibly face the vultures or stay here and wait for him? Walking into the bedroom, I expect to find him asleep. Oh, Crap! Oh Crap! I'm wrong. My heart begins to race. What if he really has left? He has a plane, what if he decided to leave Miami? Can he do that, leave that quickly? I practically run into the bathroom, coming back out through the closet into the bedroom, that's when I catch a glimpse of him, sitting in a chair looking out into the now dark sky. I walk over and stand beside him. Without saying a word, he gently takes my hand and pulls me into his lap.

Wrapping my right arm around him, I lay my left hand across his chest. Trying to find the correct words, I sigh deeply. Finding those chocolate eyes that cause me to melt, I gingerly say, "I thought you left me just now. I am so sorry, H. I had no right to say those things."

Still not saying anything, he raises his hands to cup the side of my face. Gently caressing my cheek, he leans into me when I think I hear him whisper, "Never." We sit wrapped in each other finding solace in the stillness of the room each attempting to work through this day in their own way. Standing I take him by the hand, suggesting we wash this horrible day away. With a small acknowledgement, Houston stands as I take him by the hand leading us into the bathroom. I smile as he pulls his shirt off. He knows. Damn him he knows exactly what he is doing. I always like to watch him turn the water on. For whatever the reason, I find watching this simple task very sensual. It's his finely sculpted muscles moving as one that I just can't pull myself away from.

Turning to face me with a small genuine smile spreading across his face, "I shouldn't have stayed in the office. I hadn't been back very long when Jeffrey came in. He didn't want to tell me about your day. He knew what it would do to me. I had to threaten him. Finally, he enlightened me about the things they said to you, how you looked. I was furious. Not with the scum you had to deal with but with myself. I left you without any protection. I should have known better. I just didn't think they would go after you so quickly. That's when I had a couple more shots."

Slowly undressing the other, we playfully touch. Stepping into the multi-head shower, the hot water hits us from every direction. Picking up a soft cloth, I apply body wash and move to Houston. Beginning to wash his well -defined body, no matter how many times I try, I can't pull my eyes from his. This might possibly be the most erogenous bath I will ever experience. We are tenderly washing each other, not missing one inch. With each swipe of the cloth it is as if we are wiping away all of the intenseness from earlier. All the pain we each felt during the day is flowing down the drain. Houston pulls me to him. Wrapping my arms around his neck, he grasps the back of my thighs and scoops me up in a protective embrace as if I were nothing. Taking two steps, I feel my back press against the marble wall. Leaning his forehead against mine me, he speaks. "When I read your text about the shit storm, I lost it." Pulling him tighter to me, if that is possible, the only words I can manage to squeak out are, "It's okay Houston." Standing with my legs wrapped tightly around his waist, I want to crawl inside his skin. I can't get close enough.

"No, it is not ok Charli. I was just about to enter an important meeting with men that had traveled a very long way, crossing several continents to sign contracts with Highland Diversified. I was not very pleasant. I signed the contracts, explained I had an emergency in Miami and I left them."

"Ah, ok. I really don't know how to respond to that, Houston. I regret sending you that text. Please forgive me." Frowning, just a little, he turns us around, walking out of the shower with his powerful arms wrapped underneath my backside. As I slide down his wet slick body, Houston wraps a bath sheet off the heated bar around me. He begins drying my body as gently as if he were rubbing a fragile piece of glass. Wrapping me in another warm bath sheet, he dries himself. Kissing my shoulder, patting my behind, he winks at me saying, "Go on and get something on, I want to brush my teeth."

Secretly, that makes me very happy. I don't care for the smell of whiskey. After today, I can say with fair certainty, the only way I will ever drink whiskey again is if I am out of my mind. Opening the t-shirt drawer, retrieving one for me, not knowing what we wants to put on, I pick up the remote to close it. These remote controlled drawers are amazing. I have to admit, I've wondered what would happen if there was a power outage. Smiling, shaking my head as I return it back to its place all I can think is men and their remotes. As I pull the shirt over my head, Houston enters the closet, grabs some of his favorite athletic pants, as he calls them, slips them on and gives me the once over. Shaking his head, "No. I don't think so. Are you trying to drive me crazy? There are others here, bottoms," as he moved his finger up and down. I pull out a pair of my leggings and off we go downstairs. Normally, I would put up a fight about how far his tee comes down my legs. I would point out it covers as much if not more than some of my dresses but I think it best not to push it right now. H needs to feel in control.

Chapter 23

Even though he said there were others here, I see or hear no one. We automatically go into the kitchen which is actually part of the open living space. Each of us begins pulling items for our meal. I suppose we are really hungry. Funny, neither of us realized it until we came downstairs. Our conversation is stifled somewhat. We are trying to ignore the elephant in the room. Obviously, we want, no not want because Lord knows I would like to completely wipe the entire day out of my mind, but need to discuss the day's events. Neither of us broaches the subject other than what was said upstairs.

As we eat our honey-lime grilled chicken and Greek cucumber salad, a thought suddenly hits me. "Houston, where did this food come from?" Raising his eyes to meet mine and with a quizzical look on his face, he manages to get "What?" out between bites.

"Where did this food come from?"

Pausing for a minute, a grin breaking across his once stone face, "Well, I'm not sure which poultry farm but I am sure the chicken was treated humanely, if that is your concern. The seasonings came from wherever they come from. I do know at one time in history, actually thousands of years ago, my answer might have been The Spice Islands. As for the salad…"

Stop it! You jerk." I pick up my dinner roll, contemplating if I should toss it at him. Only problem that briefly crosses my mind is what might come back at me. Lifting an eyebrow at me, he sits just watching. Smiling, I give him my what the hell look instead. "You know exactly what I mean, smartass. Where did this food come from?" I begin waving my hands above my plate as if I am some game show hostess. "I know you have some standing orders from local chefs, some of it is delivered frozen and you cook it but I mean this specific food tonight. You have been gone for over a month. I was here yesterday morning and I don't think it was here."

"It was delivered this morning, Baby." Lifting my eyebrows, with a what the hell look, I stand, pick my plate up enter the kitchen. Setting the plate on the counter, I walk to the refrigerator, jerk the door open and find it fully stocked with fresh items. "Houston?"

"Yes."

Doing my best to seem very casual, I decide to use a different plan of attack to get an actual answer. Two can play the casual game, my dear hunk. Telling myself, I am not going to be a shrew about what I just saw. Turning to the garbage disposal, I scrape my plate, and begin to wash it. "Never mind."

"I really wish you would learn to leave that. That is what I pay a considerably hefty cleaning service bill for. They come in each day and take care of the previous day's items." Walking over to the table where we ate, I look down at his plate. He must be finished so I repeat the process. "Humor me, ok? I like to feel useful and don't try to change the subject."

With as casual a voice as I'm sure he can muster, he simply states, "I'm unsure as to what subject you are referring to."

Oh, I would just love to see him in action during a business negotiation. I can only imagine how he works the group before him. "A fridge full of fresh food is the subject." Looking at him, he knows darn well what I am talking about. Standing, he takes me by the hand, guiding us to the elevator. As the elevator doors open up to a lite area, the LED lighting draws my eyes to his pool's infinity edge as we step onto the deck. Each time I stand here, looking across the pool I feel as if I am walking toward a sky full of ocean. Wait, I don't remember the lights being on earlier. How does he do that stuff? That was the last thought I had about any type of lights.

Pulling me into his arms, Houston kisses my neck finding "the spot." It's the exact spot that always reduces me to something that resembles a volcano of hot lava waiting to erupt. Pulling away, he scoops me up and carries me over to a contemporary patio chair, that I secretly call the nut chair because it reminds me of a coconut. Releasing me, I slide down his body as his hands trace my waist all the way up. (This scooping and sliding seems to be a trend tonight. A girl could get use to all this extra contact I'm experiencing.) Lowering himself down first, I casually stand watching him as he is looking at me. WOW! That is hot. Pulling me closer to him, every nerve ending within my body is screaming for him to stop undressing me with his eyes. I'd prefer if his hands took over and were moving across my body releasing me from this oversized shirt which I find is actually confining me. After a minute or two, H. pulls me into our favorite sitting position. I'm leaning back against his chest but sitting between his legs feeling his erection press against my backside. Scooting back as far as I can, a moan escapes him. Tightly, wrapping his muscular arms around me, we sit snuggling each lost in our thoughts.

With a cold, distant voice that was once passion filled, he says, "I can't do this anymore, Charli." Tensing, I try getting up but his arms tightens holding me in place.

"Why are you doing this? Let me get up Houston." Without a doubt, he can feel my response to the devastating blow he has just given me. The change in not only the position of my body but the speed with which my heart is now racing is a give-away to how that one phrase has affected me.

Taking a very deep breath, I hold it a minute. Finding the courage to ask the question flying around in my head, I exhale, "Do what Houston?" With a snarl I continue, "Please explain to me just what it is you can't do anymore. I need to know this very minute." Right now, I am thanking the good Lord above that it is dark and that I'm facing the same direction as him. He can't see the tears forming in my eyes. I have no doubt he was able to hear them in my voice. He once told me he had special people reading skills. I hope he can read me right now.

"This thing that we are doing. I'm going to ask you a question and I want you to be completely honest with me."

Nodding my head and whispering "OK." I brace my heart for whatever is coming.

"Are you happy?" he asks while keeping his arms tight around me. Before I can answer he continues in a tone I dare not interrupt. "With our situation right now? Think before you answer."

"Maybe before I answer, you should tell me your thoughts on the subject."

I feel him swallow, continuing on he says "I love you, Charli."

Interrupting him, "Love me? What the hell, Houston? You just said and I quote, I can't do this anymore. In the next couple of minutes you tell me you love me. Would you please make up your mind! Talking about mixed signals. What the…"

Next thing I know, Houston clamps his hand over my mouth. "Will you shut up woman? Let me finish! Nod your head, yes and I will remove my hand." I nod. Before he removes it, he says, "If you dare start back on that tirade I will put it right back.

Nod yes again, that you understand. I nod. Keeping his word, he removes his hand. "The past twenty-four hours have driven me crazy because the thing I knew I wasn't doing was hurting you."

Placing my hands on top of his I ask calmly, "H. what are you not doing that caused me to be hurt?"

With a distant voice I don't recognize he continues, "Keeping you safe and protected Baby. I have known for some time the paparazzi would more than likely begin to follow/aggravate you. I did nothing. I talked myself into believing that you wouldn't need a full time bodyguard. Then, you were here going through what I believe you called a "shit storm" while I was a thousand miles away. Relaxing his arms a little, I push away from him.

"Give me a minute." Standing up, I walk to the edge of the pool. Staring down into the clear water, with my back to him, I attempt to process what he said. I have faced many situations in my life where I've had to draw upon my courage. At this very moment not only am I putting together the words I need to say, but I am reaching down inside to draw on that courage to give him what he ask for.

"Charli, I asked for complete honesty." Turning to look at him with a somber face, I am trying to find the right words. Raising my hand to my necklace, I find the energy to speak. "Houston, you can't protect me. This isn't the eighteenth century where the man protects his woman and maintains a safety net around her. I really don't think it happened back then either. All that safety nonsense is just some fantasy some romantic created. This is the twenty-first century where women are responsible for their own safety; where bad things, terrible things happen sometimes. All we can do is love each other while trying to care for the other." Replacing what he probably viewed as a glum face with a smile, I continue. "I love you, too. For the record, I have hated the past month with you being away but I agree the last twenty-four hours have really sucked."

As I finish my little speech, he begins to rise. Shaking my head, I capture his eyes doing for him one of the things I know he really enjoys. I undress for him never breaking the connection we have. Continuing to hold his line of sight, I slide into the warm waters of the pool. I'm not sure when I finally realized it but at some point the understanding that this has been a really bad day for both of us has sunk in. How selfish have I been for the past twenty four plus hours? I never thought about Houston at all when I was dealing with the vultures. I didn't stop to think about how I might be upsetting him by sending those texts.

Chapter 24

Lying in bed after the pool, we both seem to feel the weight of the day has finally passed. Houston joined me in the pool earlier. We talked, laughed, swam, caressed, teased and enjoyed being together. It was as if tonight's swim was the first time we had been in the pool at night; it was different somehow from the other times. Tonight, we were a couple, not just individuals enjoying the others company. The rush of the water over our naked bodies provided an intimacy that seemed to stretch beyond any of our previous pool encounters. It is very late or very early depending on how I look at it. Whatever the time, it doesn't matter. We're together both trying to make up for the lost month when we were apart. Pulling me to him, Houston whispers into my ear the one question I can't answer.

"Will you move in here? Call Dade 303 your home, our home."

Almost as if he knew my answer would be no, he continues without giving me an opportunity to speak. "Baby, if we are going to be together, I need to know you are safe, when I'm not in town. I travel quite a bit. It's the nature of the beast called Highland Diversified. Think what the past twenty-four hours, well closer to thirty-six now have been like. Living here, those blood suckers won't have as much of an opportunity to attack you, like they will at your apartment." Turning in his arms, I snuggle in but remain silent.

Beginning to tenderly stroke my arm as if it is as much for him as it is for me, Houston breathes deeply. Continuing in a voice that could possibly be described as far away. "Let me explain something first, then, I have a confession." Opening my mouth, he quickly adds "Shh, don't say anything until I am finished. Nod your head, yes, that you agree to remain silent no matter how difficult it might be until I am completely finished." With my head on his shoulder, he could feel me nod. "Most people would describe me as an extremely focused person, especially in the office. I do not allow any distractions. Never, when I am in a meeting. Rumors have it, there are some individuals that call me brutal especially in the boardroom. Actually, I can't disagree with that line of thought. After reading your text, I couldn't focus no matter how much I tried. You have to understand, I do not allow anything to come between me and my business. I have been married to my career in one form or another for as long as I can remember. The only thing I have actually loved until very recently was my career. A woman entering into my thoughts at an HD meeting is unheard of. Highland Diversified has always come first with me. She is a very jealous lover. Those unlucky bastards yesterday were on the receiving end of my uneasiness. I can assure you I wasn't pleasant. That reminds me, I need to call the

Chinese Ambassador tomorrow to offer my apologies."

I cringe when he says Chinese Ambassador. Crap! Is he really going after world domination? "Houston, I was upset that you didn't text me back. I am sorry. I didn't know you were in a meeting with people that represent an entire country. I should never have sent it. I was very selfish. Sometimes, I forget just how powerful and influential you really are."

Squeezing me as he pulls me into him. "Charli, let me make myself absolutely clear." Taking a deep breath he continues, "I don't want what I am about to say to scare you. I have thought a great deal about this. Since meeting you, I have felt a depth of emotions that I didn't know existed for me, for others yes but not me. This is a new experience for me, feeling like this. The intensity is indescribable. The only way I can possibly begin to understand, much less explain my feelings is to say, it is as if you consume me." Opening my mouth, I begin to speak but he shakes his head, puts his finger on my lips, "Let me finish." Laying quietly in the arms of this magnificent man, I continue listening to him speak about things I am sure he has never spoken of to anyone. "I don't know where I end and you begin. Once upon a time, I would have called anyone that speaks like I am right now a damn fool. I would have said the type and depth of love I am describing doesn't exist. No matter what my feelings are, no matter how deep my love is I want you to know one thing." Placing his hand under my chin, and tilting my face up to his, I see the look on his face. A look that I am not sure, I have ever seen on anyone's face before especially when they look at me. Licking my dry lips, I manage to ask, "What is the one thing, H?"

"Baby, you will always be safe with me. I would forfeit everything I own to ensure your safety and happiness. That isn't the one thing though. Here is the one thing. If you can't be safe being with me then I will walk away from you. It would almost destroy me but I will do it. Knowing you are safe, here in our home will keep me sane when I must travel."

Wrapping my arm around him, I don't know what to say. How in the world do I respond to what he has just told me? Smiling I say in what I hope he understands is my attempt to lighten the moment, "Give me a minute to process that a man seeking world domination says he loves me. I am not sure that a minute is actually enough."

Laughing, Houston quickly replies back, "That is what you deem important from all the things that I just said? World domination? At this very minute, I can only think of dominating one person not the world as she so sassily accused me of."

Our mood is moving from seriousness to joking, which makes me happy. I like to see H. when he is happy. Unfortunately, it seems he is serious so much of the time. Rolling over and straddling his waist, I smile down at him. Yum! Finally speaking, I say, "Seriously H., I'm glad you shared all of that with me. It really is more than my mind can process at this time of night. OK?" I begin tracing over his chest. Smiling, I ask, "Why are you so adamant about me moving in here? If I continue to live at my place and just stay here when you are in town, wouldn't that be ok?"

"Where have you been? Were you not just listening to me? Woman, you drive me crazy!"

Continuing to trace on his chest, I need to feel him. "Thank you very much, Mr. Houston Donovan, I was listening."

"I don't want this to influence your decision or scare you because that is not my intent with what I am about to say but Baby you have no idea the level of some of the people I must deal with. There are some very unscrupulous people in the world especially in big business. Greed causes some individuals to do some very dangerous things sometimes. I just want to know you are safe. Want isn't the correct word. I need to know you are safe or as safe as I can keep you."

"Can't you tell me who you need to protect me from? Is it the Chinese? Would someone hurt me to get to you?"

"No, it isn't the Chinese. There are others that I don't want to discuss with you. I don't think anyone would hurt you but I **will not** take any chances. Damn woman, I won't ask again. Give me your answer."

Kissing his neck and slowly moving up to his ear, I whisper, "I have been giving it to you since I climbed on top of Mount Houston. You claim to be such an astute businessman. I thought you would have figured it out."

Laying there looking a little confused he is quiet. Then the smile came. "Very sly my luscious lady." I continued touching his chest but this time I said, "There might be a sneaky spy lurking nearby so let me write the letter Y." (I write it onto his chest.) I see a bit of a smile appearing. "I want to see, I want to see, so let me write the letter E." (I write an E onto his chest.) "So you won't have to guess, let me write the letter S." (I write an S onto his chest.) Leaning over. I whisper, "Yes."

Still sitting on top of him with my knees on the bed, I am beginning to get a little nervous. Raising his left hand to my right cheek, he caresses it as gently as one would touch a newborn lamb. I turn into this gentle yet somehow firm touch, kissing his palm. Slipping his hand to the back of my head, he guides my lips to his. The intenseness of the moment has passed as he nips my lower lip. Quickly, our playful kisses melt into a passion filled contact that spreads across our bodies. Rolling me onto my back, Houston plunges deep into me. I can only yell his name as a passion inflamed inferno causes my hips to rise up to meet his long plunging strokes. Moments later, Houston joins me on our pleasure filled cloud.

Chapter 25

As I walked into the kitchen this morning all I could do was shake my head when my eyes land on Houston looking very executive in his suit and tie. I marveled at how together he is after just a few hours of sleep. The burning ember Houston has ignited within me flared as he looked up from his orange juice giving me his megawatt smile. Sitting at the breakfast bar, he simply says, "Good Morning, Baby." I melt every time he uses that sexy tone with me. He seems to really like that little pet name. Actually, I like it when he calls me Baby, too. "Good Morning, to you also, Mr. Up and Dressed Bright n' Early. I see you are ready to face the new day in your quest for world domination."

Almost choking on his juice, he smirks, "I think world domination might be just a little extreme. Don't you?" Raising my eyebrow just a little, I shrugged my shoulders, pouring myself a glass of juice. "I'll settle for overseeing my vast empire, Ms. Jensen."

Slowly nodding my head in agreement, "It probably is a vast empire, I just don't know how vast." I leaned in with a smile and a kiss on his cheek.

Shifting the bar stool to the right, he looks at me and says, "Come here, woman. I need at least an adequate good morning and whatever that thing that you just did on my face was definitely not adequate."

Smiling, I sit my juice glass down and move to stand between his legs. Giving him a kiss that causes the burning embers I have left to burst into a full out bonfire on the beach type of heat. Between our deep throated kisses, Houston mumbles, "Damn, I have to leave for the office in about five minutes or I would sweep everything off this counter and take you right here."

Backing up and turning away, I shake my behind at him in a suggestive way. Reaching over to pick up my juice glass, I move out of his way just before his swatting hand makes contact with me. I look over my shoulder and in my best seductive voice I say, "Houston, have a wonderful day." After finishing the last bite of his bagel, he stands, giving me that dazzling smile and asks, "What are you going to do today my sexy siren?"

Smiling, I respond "I am going into the office in a couple of hours my magnificent mogul."

With a chuckle, he looks at me mumbling, "If I didn't have a conference call with the Chinese Ambassador and his delegation this morning, in under (looking at his watch) forty minutes, I would prove to you how magnificent this mogul, as you put it, can be" raising his eyebrows a couple of times quickly.

I can't help but laugh at this playful banter we are engaged in. "Don't think that all this talk about me being magnificent and this sexy walking of yours is driving my original question about your plans for

230

the day out of my mind. I must have my assistant schedule a hearing appointment for me."

Looking confused at him, I ask with genuine concern, "Why would you do that? Are you having some type of problem?"

"I didn't think so until about five seconds ago when I thought I heard you mention something about going to the office."

Giving him the oddest look, I can muster, I reply. "Forget the hearing test. You have no worries. Your hearing is just fine because that is exactly what I said. I am going into SCT in about an hour."

Crossing the room, to pick up his briefcase keeping his back to me, he says in what must be his authoritative business voice, "No, I don't think so."

My mid-west girl is busting out at her seams, as I put my hand on my hip. "Houston Donovan! I so know I didn't just hear you tell me no. You might need the hearing exam after all because I don't remember asking you." Holding my finger up as if I had experienced a revelation then pointing to myself I say, "because I **am** going into the office."

Flashing me a smile that in most instances would cause my panties to melt, he says, "Walk with me, we can pretend to discuss this. I've got to get out of here. My five minutes were up about eight minutes ago."

The jig is up (as Daddy use to say). He now knows that I'm going into the office. It's not as if I was planning on going behind his back, I just was returning to my normal routine. As we walk to the elevator together he asks me, "Has yesterday been erased from that beautiful mind of yours? What about last night's events and the conversations we had?"

Rolling my eyes, as I turn my head, "How could one of the worst days of my life simply fade away? I don't think I'll ever forget yesterday." The elevator opens, with Nash appearing all ready to go, stepping into the foyer, "Ma'am." My first thought is, about his weapon. I wonder if that's why he always wears a suit no matter how hot it is. Not a conversation for this morning. Note to self, talk to H. about the gun thing. Nodding my head and smiling, "Nash." The second thought is oops I'm in H's tee shirt with bed head. Not a pretty sight.

Taking my elbow, guiding me over with him, "Ride down with me. We can finish our discussion," Houston says entering the elevator.

Looking down at what I have on, I look back up into those chocolate wonders, "Are you kidding? I can't go outside in your tee shirt, Houston."

Clearing his throat, Nash quickly adds, "No one will see you. We are going directly to the basement, Ma'am."

Flashing him a half smile that I hope he realizes is not actually a smile but more of a gesture of gee thanks, I thank him. I have a sneaky suspicion at this very moment Nash will tell me just about anything to get Houston out of here. He knows Houston is on a tight schedule today. It is seven-thirty in the morning and already behind. He usually leaves for the office around six forty-five.

Stepping in, Houston wastes no time and jumps onto the topic. Glancing at Nash but tilting his head toward me, "She thinks she's going into the office." Making some sound that I have never heard before Nash winces. Focusing back on me H says, "Now, let's quickly discuss this. You need to rethink your plans. If they know where both you and Lana live don't you think they know about your office? How will you get anything finished? Will it be a productive day for Supreme Corporate Travel if you are in the office? Let me answer that for you in case you might be confused, no it will not be productive and yes, they know about the office. Am I correct Nash?"

Never moving a muscle, Nash answers, "Yes, they do. Several of them camped out across the street most of the night. One of my men has alerted me that the numbers are growing."

Sighing deeply, "First off, they don't know where I live because I live here now, right? So the joke is on them." I say with a fake little laugh.

Houston glances over at me with his your pushing it look. All he said was, "Yes, you do. Be reasonable."

His words are hit me like another ton of bricks, one last night and now one today. Darn those bricks, I'm glad they're imaginary. I'm not being reasonable I'm being stubborn. It will be best for Supreme Corporate Travel, and for me, if I stay away. Probably for a few days at least. I took a deep breath, "You're right, I will stay away from the office. I'll go over and begin packing my things."

Stepping out of the elevator, Houston turns and says "Charli! Did you simply forget our safety conversation? You will do no such thing. You'll stay right here in the penthouse today far away from your apartment. It might not be safe if you were to be seen entering your building. You saw and heard what those story hounds are like."

Giving him my best puppy dog look, I say "Ok, H. You're right."

"Houston." Nash says as he gets into the SUV.

Holding up his hand, "I know I am. I know Nash, I'm late but I'm going to be just a little later he says as he steps back into the elevator and smiles.

Chapter 26

It's been a little over two weeks since I officially moved into Houston's penthouse. I've been here most nights for months, well the months he was in town, but now the penthouse at Dade 303 is my home, our home. I really can't describe what these two words do to me, our home. How they make me feel. There was a time when, I thought I would never be able to live on my own again, much less share a home with someone. When I think of Houston Donovan as being my someone I get a warm feeling all over. I still haven't researched him. There is nothing floating around out in cyberspace that I want to know. Smiling, I pull my necklace out from under my silk blouse and toy with the heart pendant. What I know is right here in my heart, my beating heart. I know that he has been running Highland Diversified from his Miami office for the past couple of weeks. He has even mentioned hiring a domestic staff for 303 and making this his permanent home. I must admit that makes me very happy.

He has been here for me since what I have come to refer to as "the attack of the vultures" but I know this can't last much longer. I dread the time that is quickly coming when he will fly off to visit another of his major corporate offices. The last couple of days, I've picked up on some very subtle hints about me going with him. Just the thought of that causes my pulse to race. My comprehension of the accident is still lacking. How can I make him understand, I can't go with him because of something that happened ten years ago? I dread the conversation we must have about my flying and my fear. That's a conversation for another day. Leaning back in my new office chair that Lana and Joan surprised me with this morning, I must admit it is good to be back at Supreme Corporate Travel. No matter how connected I stayed during my work from home it wasn't the same. All the video chatting, working in real time with Lana or retrieving info from the cloud is just not the same as sitting behind my desk in my office. It is good to sit here and to actually feel a part of the SCT family. Well, as much as you can feel a family when you are a family of three. I know how that feels both in my real family and my work family, to be part of a trio. Strange number for me to associate with families, three. Hmm, is my family really three or is H a part of it? Then it is four. I wonder what he would say if I ask him, "Do you consider us family?" Smiling, I can hear him in my head, "Baby, what the hell? Of course we're family." Then he would pull me into his arms.

I am lost in thinking about what we would be doing with our bodies when I hear a noise. Glancing over at the door, Lana is standing there just looking at me. "Lana did you just clear your throat to get my attention?" Shaking her head at me. "Girl, you got it bad. Yes. I came in here to see if you are about ready for lunch? What I find is you staring off into space with that goofy smile. I must admit it is good to see that smile on your face."

"Ok smarty, what goofy smile are you talking about?"

"It's that smile you get when you are in love. It also tells me you weren't focusing on that open folder right in front of you. Course if I had what you have waiting for you tonight then I'd have that smile too." Completing changing the subject, she adds, "Hey, I want us to zip over to a little sandwich shop on Ocean that I found last week. I didn't tell you about it, did I?" Pushing back from my desk, I say, "No. You've been holding out on me."

"Just wait till you try one of their Specials piled high with… What in the world is that playing? Is that your phone?"

"Don't roll your eyes at me Lana. Yes, that's my phone. It's Houston's text tone. I'll check it in a minute. That place on Ocean Drive sounds good to me." Turning to walk out of my office, I hear her say "Sure, you'll check it in a minute. Yeah, that minute is about up."

How's your day?
Good!
You've worked some?
Yes, accomplished lots, actually.
Yours?
Working toward world domination

Lucky world☺

Going out for lunch?

I knew it! You're checking on me. Yes going with Lana somewhere on Ocean.

Kirk is out front. He'll drive you. No discussion.

Alright. Did u notice, no discussion?

Good girl.

I don't like being good. Remember?

Stop. I have work I must do.

I could come to you and we could be bad together! Lana will understand. Missing my mid-day "feast of u"

Baby! UR Killing me.

Finding a good stopping place, we head to lunch. Lana turns to head to the front but stops when I say, "Kirk is out back waiting."

Predictable as ever, Lana rolls her eyes saying "Kirk?" just about the time she raises her hand in some weird questioning gesture. Joan says, "Ah, actually he is in the spare office we're using for storage. I believe he is on his laptop or something like that."

Lana being Lana makes a smart remark, "You've heard of the old movie, Invasion of the Body Snatchers, well we've got Invasion of Houston's Men right here in our office. He must have heard us because Kirk stepped out of the spare room, "Ma'am."

238

Acknowledging him I say "Kirk, we want to eat at a sandwich place over on Ocean Drive."

"Yes Ma'am." Walking to the back door, he hesitates before he opens it and says, "Give me a couple of minutes to check things and get her started." Smiling, I nod. "Ok."

Lana looks at me with big eyes, she says "Mother of Mercy! Get her started? Did he just really say that? Ah, he can start me anytime! Charli, is the requirement to work for Houston that all his men must be hotter than sin?"

Laughing as we walk out the back door, H's signature navy blue Mercedes rolls to a stop. Kirk gets out as Lana reaches for the door but I stop her. Leaning over to her I whisper, "I've learned one thing, they don't like it when I open the door. I think it's a male thing. Just wait."

Quickly enclosed in the back of the car, we speed off to lunch. I'm sure he uses some navigation system but Kirk takes us to Lana's shop on Ocean without one wrong turn. It's good to be with Lana, be out in the city and enjoying my freedom. We're joking about the way several tourist are dressed when Houston sends me another text. Lana just looks at me and laughs when my ring tone plays.

Your kisses lift me higher,
Like the sweet song of a choir you light my morning sky,

With burning love.

Looking back at her, I smile saying,"Whaaat? It's Houston. It's a joke between us."

Giving me a you've got it bad look all she said was, "Joke, right. It better be Houston. That's all I've got to say."

"Who else in the world would it be?"

We sat in silence enjoying our sub sandwiches.

"Just one more question, Charli. Then I promise not to say anything else."

"OK, what?"

Did you have to select *Burning Love*?"

Almost choking on my drink, I look at Lana, "How do you know this song? It is old."

Yep, it's old alright. I learned it from my Grandmother. She used to play it all the time when I would stay with her. We would dance around her living room and sing it at the top of our lungs. Apparently, it was hers and my Grandfather's song."

"Well, just goes to show you, I've got good taste."

"Yeah, have you seen that man you are living with? What was the term some woman called him? Liquid gold? Liquid sex? No, maybe it was liquid gold sex? Hum?"

Covering my red face with both my hands, I just shake my head refusing to make any comments.

It was really nice to be able to move through my day without having one of the vultures following me. I suppose some scandal involving some notorious celebrity has broken and boring little me has been dumped. Good riddance!

When Lana and I enter the office, Joan is extremely cheerful. I move on back to my office and just as I was about to open the door, Joan hands me a manila envelope saying, "This came for you while you were out. I noticed it is labeled urgent." Taking it from her, I turned to open my door. Just about the time *Burning Love* began playing from my bag causing Joan to throw up her hands, "I am not asking." With that remark she returns to her desk. I open my door, enter my office, sit down at my desk and finally extinguish the fire my phone was singing about.

Good Lunch?

Yes.

Working later than planned. Expect a call from Ashley in a bit. She has a surprise for you.

Who?

Assistant

Interesting use of personnel!

I have connections

I like a man with them. ;)

Personnel or Connections?

Connections.

C U Baby

Counting on seeing all of U, H.

I dive into my accounts, Ashley goes on the back burner. Joan buzzes me, letting me know my four thirty appointment has arrived. I quickly check my calendar. I have no clue as to who she is referring to. Curious, I stand and walk to the front.

"Ms. Jordan?"

"Yes."

Walking toward me with a smile that screams I'm faking my happiness, is a short (shorter than my 5'6"), blonde woman, sunglasses perched on top of her head, dressed in a pantsuit that would rival the red of a springtime tulip. She is holding a clipboard. How strange!

I know immediately this is Ashley way before she can introduce herself.

Extending her hand, "Ashley Smithson, I believe Mr. Donovan contacted you to let you know to expect me." As we shook hands, I respond in a manner that conveys the confusion I am feeling, "I was under the impression, I would receive a phone call."

"Phone call, goodness gracious no. Ms. Jordan, you are joking surely?"

Squinting my eyes just a little, "Well, maybe I am." I turn to look at Joan who is standing with her lips pressed together trying to contain her laughter.

"Never squint Ms. Jordan, never squint. You'll regret it, when you are my age."

Looking over at a closed door, she says "Now, I have set up in your tiny, little conference room. I hope that is alright for you."

Glancing over at Joan, Ashley hustles me into what was once our conference room. I am sure Joan can read the "What the…" as Ashley opens the door. Oh my God! I mouth to Joan as I look over my shoulder. Ashley is correct this room appears tiny. Actually, it isn't as small as it feels at this very minute but with the covered racks of what I assume is clothing, at least it looks like clothing racks, I do feel a little claustrophobic. If those things covered up are indeed types of clothing, then I know or assume those smaller boxes are coordinating shoes. As I walked further into the room, I stop, turn and ask, "You don't work for Houston, do you?"

"Gracious, no. I am the executive assistant to, Deniel Foss."

"Excuse me, Deniel Foss as in D. Foss Designs?"

"Yes Ma'am, the one in the same."

With a sigh she continues, "Mr. Donovan has requested I outfit you in a special cocktail dress for the evening. Since, I am unfamiliar with your tastes/likes I brought an array of choices. Next time I will be more familiar with your style." With a twinkle in her eye, she hints that these are the crème de la crème.

Next time? I really have so many things to learn or get use to about Houston's world. I am not sure if my attempt at casualness, as if this type of thing happened every day, is working but I'm giving it my all. I can only imagine what Ashley is thinking as I continue my statue impression.

"Ms. Jordan."

"Shaking my head, Jensen. Charli Jensen. I've had several people do that lately. I must look like my last name should be Jordan."

Suddenly, Ashley's face looks as if, it has been seized by a character in a horror movie. "Please, forgive me Ms. Jensen. I am very sorry. My client earlier today was a Jordan." Laughing nervously, she continues, "Today seems to be my J day. I had a sudden lapse in memory. Please do not hold this against me. Please do not mention this to Mr. Donovan."

Closing my eyes, inhaling/exhaling slowly all I could think was this poor woman. "Ashley, it's okay. You just made a simple mistake."

"Thank you, Ma'am. If I may say so, some of our clients would be very upset if I made that mistake and called them by the wrong last name. In fact, so upset that I would be dismissed from the site that very moment. Mr. Foss would already have been called. Thank you again."

Smiling, I simply said, "Good grief. It was a mistake. It is already forgotten."

With a less superior attitude, Ashley guides me over to the racks as her assistant uncovers the first one. Standing in awe, my eyes are moving so swiftly they can barely focus. Every color of the rainbow is hanging in front of me. WOW! Then we began a process that I soon realize is just a little more complicated than me moving among the racks.

"Ms. Jensen, let's begin with some basic questions." Looking from the first rack to the second I have to ask, "Does that rack have dresses also?"

"No, that is our coordinating lingerie. We will uncover it after you have selected your dress." Slowly nodding my head in a trance like fashion I respond, "Well, OK then."

"I know isn't it wonderful? You are very lucky to have a man like Mr. Donovan, if I man say so. I am sure all the items I have brought for you today will please him."

Smiling, thinking to myself, what happened to pleasing me? I suppose in this world, the person footing the bill is the person that should be pleased. I agree that H will like them, "Let's get started, shall we?" I answer what feels like a million questions. With what I almost describe as a glow, Ashley guides me to a dress she believes is the one for tonight. Responding to her choice I say, "Ashley, it's fabulous, I agree." Slowly the glow dims. She knows what I am about to say. "It's not for me though but I do see the one." The navy, mini with the sweetheart neckline is where I stop.

She's glowing again. "Oh, Ms. Jensen nice choice. Yes, the A line will look great on you. I have no idea where you are going tonight but these glittering crystals will sparkle under the lights."

Apparently Houston wants me to have the full Ashley experience so I want the full experience as well. She turns, discusses something with her assistant, within what seems like a minute or two, the lingerie the dress requires is being handed to her. Looking to me she says, "Please understand the selections for your lingerie are completely based upon your selection. Because the dress has a band across the back and so much of your skin will be showing, there is no bra to compliment the gown. Holding up the first selection, I shake my head. "No, I don't care for thongs." The second choice is a pair of navy, lace and satin boy shorts. Smiling, I say, "Yes." I know Houston will love the snug fitting sheer-tulle hips. I am getting a little heated just thinking about wearing these for him. Before Ashley makes any comments, several pairs of shoes are uncovered. The shoe selection is easy, navy, satin, four inch heels, Ferragamos. I turn to leave the conference room.

"Ms. Jensen, where are you going?"

"Ahh, my office."

Standing there looking at me as if she might be preparing for battle, Ashley continues, "Oh no.

You must try the dress and shoes to ensure proper fit. I have a seamstress at the ready if anything should be required."

Both Ashley and the assistant are standing and just looking at me. (My Midwest girl is fighting to escape. She's thinking, Oh hell no! I'm not stripping my clothes off right here in the conference room.) Sensing my uncertainness, Ashley speaks very genuinely, "I can assure you Ms. Jensen, you should not feel modest in any form. We are very comfortable with women changing in front of us."

"Ashley, you may be comfortable with it but I am not. I am just going to step into our restroom."

"Perhaps we can step out giving you the room. Would that be better for you?" Nodding my head, the room quickly clears.

Changing into this gorgeous dress, I hear a light rap on the door, "May I come in?"

Managing to mumble out a "Yes" I stand here as if I am on display in a storefront window.

"Stunning! Simply stunning!" Nodding her head as she walks around me, she continues, "Oh Ms. Jensen, you were correct with the choice."

I look at Ashley with a mischievous grin and added, "Houston will like it." Along with what is and isn't underneath.

After changing, I attempt to work. I give up. Gathering my things, I leave my office. Stopping at Joan's desk, she says, "I have been wondering when you were going to stop pretending you were actually getting some work completed. Go home, relax. I have a sneaky suspicion you might need some extra energy tonight."

Sticking my tongue out at her, I ask, "Do I have a driver?" Oh man, I can't believe I just asked that.   Joan nods her head and says, "out front." Deciding to tell Lana I'm checking out early, well earlier than planned, I step into her office. All she says is, "I hope you have difficulty walking tomorrow. As a matter of fact, I expect you to be in bed recuperating from tonight for most of tomorrow. So, I'll see you Thursday."

"What can I say to that, my friend?"

Smiling, her devious little smile, "Nothing, so out." Motioning with her hands for me to leave, she repeats, "Get out of here and enjoy Megabucks."

Exiting the front of the building, I realize I haven't driven since the vulture attack. That is ok because I really don't miss driving on these speedways of disaster. They are crazy here! Taking a taxi isn't much better. So, I have become a lady of leisure when it comes to driving. I am pleasantly surprised when I find the Mercedes parked out front. Exiting the sedan, Jeffery removes the dress bag from my arms, places it in the trunk returning for my remaining packages. As he opens the rear door for me, I decide to ask him something that has been eating at me for a-while. Standing between the open door and the seat, I forge ahead.

"Thank you Jeffery."

"You're welcome, Ma'am. Next time, let me know and I'll carry any packages you have for you."

Chuckling just a little, "Jeffery, can I ask you something?"

"Yes, Ma'am."

"I actually have a trick question for you."

"Ma'am?"

"What do you think I did about carrying things before I began seeing Houston? Who do you think carried my packages and drove me around?"

Tilting his head slightly, he barely raises his eyebrows but I understand his message.

Getting into the back seat, I glance up before he closes the door, "Just so you know, I am capable of doing things for myself."

"I have no doubt about that Ms. Jensen. Houston wants things done for you."

"I admit, I don't mind the not driving but sometimes I know you have better things to do than babysit me."

"Ma'am, we have a job and our job is to complete the assignments Houston gives us."

"One more thing, Jeffery. How did you end up working for Houston?"

"I knew someone that knew someone, Ma'am" shrugging his shoulders.

"Well, not exactly what I expected."

In a mimic of Jeffery's actions I shrug, "Actually it is exactly what I should have expected.

"Another man of little words." Jeffery closes the door and walks to the driver's side. As we were pulling away from the curb, he looks back at me in the mirror, "Any other place you want to go, Ms. Jensen?" "No, I don't have any other place. Thank you."

"You're welcome, Ma'am."

"Ok, Jeffery, one more thing. Please stop it with the Ma'am and Ms. Jensen. Please call me Charli. You call Houston by his first name."

"Ma'am, calling you by your first name is one thing I will never do. Thank you for the offer."

"Why, Jeffery?"

With a smirk, he answered, "Excuse, my reaction, but I like my job. I like working for Houston and I would like to continue to work for him."

"I only ask you to call me by my first name. We are spending quite a bit of time together, since you drive me more than the others but somehow I don't think you're just my driver are you, Jeffery? Please be honest."

With somewhat of a sigh he answered. "No, Ma'am, honestly I'm not. Houston wants to be sure you are safe. That incident with the paparazzi worried him. Probably more than he is willing to admit to anyone even himself."

"Thanks for your honesty, Jeffery."

Glancing into the mirror again, Jeffery smiles. "Your welcome, Charli." I returned his smile "Do you carry a weapon?"

Glancing back with a wrinkled brow, he doesn't answer for a minute. Just before we enter the parking garage, he says, "More than one, Ma'am." Sensing the topic is making him very uncomfortable, I let it drop. Helping me upstairs with my packages, I am just happy to be home. That thought hits me pretty hard. I sit down on the sofa to absorb the revelation, I just experienced. As I sit here, Jeffery returns from taking my things upstairs and hands me an envelope. I immediately recognize the writing on the front as Houston's.

Charli

"If you don't need anything else or are not planning on leaving for a while, I will head over to Highlands, Ma'am.

Looking up from the envelope, I smile and answer, "No Jeffery, I don't need anything. Thanks. Before, you say anything, I know, if I need to go anywhere I'll let you know."

Chapter 27

I sit here turning the envelope in my hands, looking at Houston's writing. The weight and texture of the paper remind me of the cards that were inside my packages. Those same cards are now tucked in the small box in my lingerie drawer. Reaching up to my neck, and touching the antique pendant, I smile. That small box held this necklace that never leaves my neck. Even though, Houston gave me this necklace, I can't think of it as mine. I see it's as a loan, the way some jewelers lend expensive pieces to certain individuals. Touching Nigel's symbol of love, it seems as if Penelope has loaned this stunning piece to me.

I have a sneaky suspicion as to what I will find. Opening the envelope, I'm not surprised to find a set of directions. Holy cow! We are really celebrating my return to the work world. Hump, I need to grab a bite to eat if we aren't going out until ten which by South Beach standards is early.

To Do List:
*Go upstairs.
*Enjoy a long hot bath to relax.
*Take a power nap. You're going to need it for tonight
*Do whatever it is you do to make yourself beautiful

*Jeff will pick you up at 9:00.

Entering the bathroom, I notice another note. This one propped on top of what has become my vanity. Same stationary with I love you scrawled on it. I smile to myself, open the bottom drawer adding this to the other notes. This is one little routine we have gotten into that I hope we never break. Leaving notes for each other, on plain little scraps of paper sometimes, tucked in all kinds of places. No place is safe. Taking out my Siren Red lipstick, I move over to his vanity, and write I can't wait to "sex you." Happy with myself, I turn to the bathtub to start the water.

I still am amazed at this custom designed Italian tub. The position of this glass tub against the outside wall just below the window makes me feel as if I am bathing in the clouds. The first time Houston and I bathed together, we had enough space to "sex each other" in the clouds. I hate that four letter f word so I adapted and found that using the term "sex me," conveyed the same meaning but just on a little higher level. When I do just want to sex Houston, I feel so comfortable sharing that thought.

Turning the water on, pouring in just a little of the exclusive bubble bath that made several celebrity most favorite lists during last Christmas, I examine the shape of the tub. The glass side and ends of the tub fascinate me. The lounger insert for the bottom transforms it into, what the Italian designer described as being, a wellness experience rather than a bath. As the gigantic tub fills, I decide to have some wine. Walking downstairs to the wine room, just off the kitchen, I select a bottle along with a glass, returning to the bathroom I think about how the wine room blows me away every time I enter it. Hearing Burning Love echoing throughout the bathroom, I pick up my pace. Walking over to answer, I think about how wonderful he is. I can get lost in his eyes.

Answering with, "How's the world domination going?"

Houston laughs. "Baby, the only dominating I want to concentrate on right now is how to dominate you."

"Houston, I can think of multiple ways."

"Where are you on the to do list?"

Smiling, I know where he is taking this conversation. "Well, I've deviated from the list just a little."

"Whatttt? Charli, I can't imagine you not doing exactly as you are directed. You seldom go off course."

Laughing, I reply with a quick, "Nope not me, never."

"What did you do, sexy lady?"

With a fake deep sigh, "Ok, I must admit. I went down to the wine closet/cellar, grabbed a bottle along with a glass. I returned to the bathroom and that's when I heard my phone.

"Well, I suppose I can excuse that. Actually, I am surprised I omitted it. That was not much of a deviation from the list. I think I am going to invoke a new rule."

"OH really? What will that be H.?"

"Well, your punishment for deviating from my list should be" pausing for a dramatic effect, "hum let me think, I'll have an idea later tonight." With a brief pause, Houston says, " Sorry Baby, I've got to take this call on my office line."

After our quick conversation is over, I decide to turn on a little music, I grab my player out of the closet. By the time, I am back, Houston has sent me a request for a video call. I accept.

"Hey, I see you are not in the tub yet."

"Nope, just getting ready to get in; the water's almost high enough for me now."

"Baby, I have another to do list but it's short."

"OK. What?"

"Walk over to your vanity. Prop the phone up. Undress for me. After you undress, turn, walk away and get into the tub. I want to watch you bathe for just a couple of minutes. Then, I'll hang up." Smiling, I do as Houston ask. I fall asleep while I am having my wellness experience/bath and don't wake until I'm getting cold. I have no idea when he hung up, I notice when I get out the call has been disconnected.

Next, on the list is to get dressed. I enter the closet/dressing room and open the lingerie. After, my makeup is applied, I decide to go ahead and put my dress on. I have about an hour or so before I am to meet Houston which means Jeffery will be here in approximately twenty minutes. I walk over to the mirror to give a final check before I head downstairs. My A-line, navy, mini dress is perfect. The sweetheart neckline accents "the girls' perfectly. H. will like my choice. Turning to my shoes, I decide not to put them on until I am downstairs. Picking up the small beaded clutch, I slip my items inside and head into the bedroom. I am almost to the door when faintly I hear a text from Houston. Looking around, I realize, I've left my phone in the bathroom.

Something's come up. Jeffery can't come. Called you a taxi? Don't like it but want you with me.

Frowning, as I reply *OK. Used cabs Before you. No big deal. See You Soon.*

Really, I don't understand what the big deal is. No one has approached me since the vultures. I do know, however, that there have been some long range pics of us that have shown up on the internet. At least that is what Lana told me today at lunch. I could care less how many long range photos they take as long as they stay away from me, us.

Thanks for understanding.
It's ok.

Chapter 28

Slipping my four inch pumps on, I stop to check the mirror on the way to our elevator. I'm ready to celebrate. Listen to me, our elevator. When the door opens in the lobby, I am thinking about how different my life is now from what it was six months ago. How accustomed I've become to the water exhibit in the lobby. How our elevator travels nonstop from the garage to the penthouse. How I just called this same elevator mine. Exiting the building, I find what appears to be a new taxi waiting. I think Houston probably requested either a new or as close to new vehicle as possible. Always the worrier, I wouldn't be a bit surprised if it has some type of bullet proof exterior since I have a normal driver. Shrugging, I know Houston always plans ahead so I am shocked that I don't have one of his "protectors" for the short drive to the office.

> *On my way. C ...U ... N ... a bit.*
> *Waiting.*
> *Did U request new taxi for me?*
> *Perhaps.*
> *FYI...I got one.*

The taxi pulls up to the Highland's building, I feel a little overdressed but it is Miami, after all. I have no doubt I'm not the first to enter this building in a cocktail dress. Starting to swipe my card the driver assures me, the fare has been prepaid. Rolling my eyes, I laugh just a little as I close the door. I check in with the night watchman on duty. "Charli Jensen. I'm seeing Houston Donovan."

"Oh, yes Ma'am. Mr. Donovan put you on the list."

"That's good? To be on the list, I mean."

As a matter of fact, you've been on the list to have access anytime for quite a few months."

Smiling, "Thanks, that's good to know."

"Let me show you over to the elevator. You will take the third set it takes you directly upstairs to the Highland main floor. Anytime, you want to do that, Ma'am, you will need the keycard for that elevator. If you don't have one, the person at the desk can always key you up."

"Ok, thank you."

"Yes, Ma'am. Anytime."

I step inside, he sends me on my way. When I step out, the main lights on the floor are dim. The logo for Highland Diversified is etched into the glass entrance wall. I stand and look at the rolling hills, wondering how many people know they represent Scotland. Shrugging my shoulders, pushing the door open, I walk into the office for the first time. I've stayed away on purpose. I don't want to be the woman that pops in and disturbs her man. Those types make me sick. He is a very busy person with a huge number of people that depend on him and the decisions he makes. Besides, I have a business myself to focus on.

I can't wait to see him sitting behind his desk. At least, I hope he is sitting behind it. I've imagined what I could do to him while he is leaning back in his soft leather chair. I'm sure it is a soft leather one. Knowing H. it might be made out of some special type of leather, something exotic like goat hide from the highest peaks of some mountain in Asia. Chuckling at myself, I stop for just a minute to try to decide where to go. Down at the end of the hall to my left, I see my destination.

So, this is the outer office of where the world domination is being plotted. Walking toward the office that I feel is his, I select the door that is cracked just a little allowing the light to shine through. Pausing for a moment before I enter into the inner sanctum, I do the check. Blowing my breath into my hand, smells fine. Next, I run my hands down my dress just smoothing out anything that might not belong. I adjust the girls since I have no bra, I want them to be in the correct place. Smiling, I push open the door. From the minute, I enter the room I'm positive this is Houston's office. It's a spacious room, with his signature navy and cream furnishings.

The end wall closest to his two tone wood desk, is mainly monitors. A couple still running stations from around the globe, China (I think.),

Australia and France. On the other side of the room is a small, conference table with eight cream leather conference chairs. Papers, folders and two laptops are on the table. It's definitely a workspace that shows signs of being utilized. Opposite the conference table, is a small sitting area overlooking the city, which includes a navy sofa with cream piping and two cream chairs. With my back to the room, I am standing at the end of the conference table. My mind is wondering if the wood is teak. A side door behind the desk opens. Smiling, I'm eager to see that fantastic man waiting for me. My hands are itching to touch him. Commenting on the office. "Houston, your office is everything I expected it to be." Leaning over and running my hand across the end, I ask "Can you sex me on this table? I mean, is it sturdy enough?

Turning to face the small noise across the room, I hear a strange voice ask, "Is it sturdy enough? What do you think? Would he have anything other than the best? Of course, it could hold you up. What was it you said?" My eyes increase to the size of the silver half dollars my mama collected when I was a little girl. Standing in the room by H's desk is a woman that is as thin as a runway model and just about as tall as one. She actually looks familiar. Is she a model that I might have seen in a magazine?

With a condescending, nails on the chalkboard voice she continues, "Oh, it was "sex me" wasn't it?

How quaint!" Following her snide comment with a hollow laugh, we stand eyeing each other.

"Where is Houston?" I ask but get no answer.

Walking over to H's desk, she picks up an ink pen, looks at it as she is turning it. Watching her actions, I have no idea why she is doing this. I am beginning to wonder if she has gone off the deep end. Putting my hand on my hip, I say, "Ok, let's try a different one then, if that one is too difficult for you. Who are you?"

She may be beautiful, tall and thin but she is strange. Drawing her eyes away from the pen, she just stands looking at me. Her eyes dart around the room and finally land on the sitting area. Something is wrong. I just know it. I've got that feeling like my skin is crawling. I haven't had this feeling in a long time. A slow almost sickening smile, crosses her face as she motions to the seating area, ignoring my questions she finally speaks, "Let's go over, and get more comfortable. I think we need to have a little girl talk."

Girl talk. "Why in the world would I have girl talk with someone I have never laid eyes on?" I ask just as snippy as this bitch was.

The smile on her face seems to be growing. It is causing my heart to pound. That phrase, girl talk, didn't help either. What do I have in common with her? My body moves on autopilot to the sofa. I sit down on the edge as she sits on one of the cream

261

lounge chairs across from me, leans back, crosses one long leg over the other, and smiles that eerie sickening smile. I can't get past the hair. (My Midwestern girl side of me thinks it looks like a "do it yourself "dye job from a box she picked up from the drug store. My city girl side understands it probably cost several hundred dollars because no one would walk around with a shade of red that looks the way it does unless it was intentional.) Trying to watch her closely while casually looking around the room, I ask, "Where did you say Houston is?"

Laughing, a weird little laugh, and flicking her wrist as if I should know the answer this strange woman says, "I didn't say but he's gone home."

I can feel my pulse racing. I start to stand as I ask, "Gone home? Why would he do that? He told me to meet him here." I can actually hear my heart beating. It may pound right out of my chest. Not wanting this stranger to see what is happening to me I am desperately trying to maintain control of myself. Oh my god, is this one of those people that H. tried to warn me about? Trying to remain calm, I lean against the back of the seat. My mind is racing. How in the world can I get in touch with him? If he has gone home then maybe I should try Jeffery because Nash would be with H.

As my eyes run over what I call a gaudy outfit which means it's probably some big name designer, I manage to mumble out of a mouth that feels as if it is

262

filled with big, fat, puffy, cotton balls, "Who are you and what are you doing in here?"

With just a little hint of a smile that some might say is almost devious shrugging her left shoulder she finally answers, "I suppose I've kept the suspense long enough, continuing with that sick smile of hers she actually leans over to shake my hand. My name is Penny."

Does this lunatic actually believe I am going to shake her hand? What if she really has a mental problem? Should I humor her? Deciding that I should, I stretch my hand to meet hers. "Charli."

Continuing, she says, "I'm not surprised that you haven't heard anyone use my name. Around Houston and his band of merry men, it is like I don't exist." With a sneer she asks, "I'm right, aren't I? You have never heard of me have you?"

At this very moment, I am seriously considering how great it would be to smack that look off of her face. "No, I haven't." is just about all I can manage. Taking several deep breathes I ask "How did you say you got into Houston's office?"

I start to stand, it suddenly dawns on me, that maybe I shouldn't be sitting here with her. What if she really is someone Houston has tried to warn me about? Obviously, she knows things about H. I am trying to remember the layout of the room and talk to this Penny person. My eyes dart around the room looking at what I can see which really isn't much

263

since I am facing the window. Attempting to use the reflection of the room to develop an escape route, in case I need it, I hope my growing fear isn't showing. Looking her directly in the eye, I know I have seen her before. Think! Was she with the paparazzi vultures? I don't think so but I could be wrong. I feel like she's vaguely familiar for some reason. "Has Houston really gone home?"

"I'll ask the questions, missy." As she shakes her finger at me, she continues on "For your information, yes, he really has gone home. Well not home but to the penthouse because home is in New York."

The more she speaks it is evident that she knows a great deal about Houston. I wonder if she is someone from his past? She must be.

Enduring her rambling, I sit here doing my best to keep her talking which gives me an opportunity to think. She spouts out, "If I was a betting girl, I'd bet that he went home to you or at least he thought he was going home to you." With a shrill laugh, she resumes her rattling, "Oh wait, I am a betting girl so I would have won that bet if I'd had money laid down on it. Damn! Just my luck." With a shrug of her right shoulder, she starts again. "I stopped him from doing that, didn't I?"

"Doing what?" I ask.

"Are you really that stupid that you can't keep up with the conversation? My goodness, his standards are falling. You can call him but I think you will want to hear what I have to say before you do."

With a look of confusion, all I can do is sit and try to piece things together, why her face seems familiar. How she knows H. Am I in danger? Think, Charli, think. The bad feeling is easing away. Normally, I would be glad about that but the bad is being replaced with fear.

She can read me. I had no idea I am so transparent. "Don't be afraid. I really didn't mean to *scare* you. Here is the way this is going to happen. We ARE going to have our little talk. Then, what you do with the information you learn is of little consequence to me. I do hope for your own sake that you have enough sense to run away when we are finished."

Penny looks at me, "I thought it was time we met. So, I came to Miami. I don't know how to say this any other way than to just come out and tell you, Houston does not love you. He might have thought he loved you for just a little while but he doesn't."

If all she really wants to do is talk and she isn't planning on hurting me, I do not have to sit here and listen to this. Making my decision quickly, I realize she isn't worth any type of physical contact. (If I ever touch her, my Midwest girl that learned to defend herself against her two brothers might take over. Then, I might end up incarcerated.) Standing up, I can't decide if I want to attack her or escape this horrible place. I walk toward the door. I don't have to listen to this crazy woman. Stopping, I draw my shoulders up to give myself all the stature possible, turn and give her a scathing look.

With that I address her in a tone that I hope matches my facial expression. "Listen! I have no idea why, *you think,* you control who Houston loves or doesn't love but let me assure you, you don't know anything about me or my relationship with him. You are wrong. He does love me."

Looking me up and down, her gaze rests on my chest. With shrieking laughter, she retorts, "I see you have a copy of my necklace." Reaching up, to caress the piece of jewelry that means so much to me, I stand trying to draw strength from the love Nigel and Penelope shared.

"Let me guess, he gave it to you while you were sitting somewhere romantic between his legs leaned back against his chest. I also bet that he had just finished a romantic story about Nigel and Penelope."

Stunned, I move my head in acknowledgement. I manage to utter, "Yes." What she just said makes the small pit in my stomach suddenly become a crater.

"No!"

Did I just yell the word no out or was it in my head? Standing there, my mind is working in overdrive. No, no, no. Pull yourself together. There is an explanation. Don't do this. I feel like I am going to be sick.

With a snarl, and a wicked grin that would please the devil himself, she asks, "You've figured it out, haven't you? Or at least a small piece of the story."

"It's not a quirk of fate, is it?" I ask turning away from her as the bile rises in my throat. It is taking every ounce of my energy to keep my hands from flying to my mouth. I will NOT run away. After all the hell I have been through I learned one very important thing about myself, I don't run. Somewhere way down inside me, I begin to call on the courage from years past. I can do this. Think about my feelings for him. Big deal this bitch knows things. I know how he makes me feel. Apparently, both of us have secrets. It's not like I have shared the things from my past. How can I judge without hearing from him?

Drawing on my inner strength, I face her with a look that I hope scares her. My icy, cold eyes (at least I hope they are) are meeting hers. Sneering at me she responds quickly, "OOOO, quick to deduce, good skill. You are going to need it. Especially, if you think you are going to travel in these circles. Let me give you a tip, learn to mask your feelings. Now, why don't you come back over here, sit down and we can finish our conversation."

Standing in the middle of his office, I'm deliberating my next action. The thing I want to happen is to wake up from this sickening nightmare. That's it, this is one of my horrible nightmares. I'll wake up any minute. Contemplating my next action, for a second or so, I walk back to the navy sofa and sit down.

"Excellent, you need to hear what I have to say. He isn't the man you think he is. Let me guess, the Houston you know is kind, caring," raising her eyebrows "a considerate lover, one that makes you wonder where he has been all your life. He puts your needs first doesn't he? You thank the powers that be that he came into your life."

I will not let her see what she is doing to me. I manage to stammer an agreement. I really don't know what I am saying. I am attempting to conceal my actual attitude. Obviously, I need to hear what she has to say no matter how it is breaking me inside. If I've learned one thing in life, in order for me to rise from the ashes of whatever this is that is happening, I must take on the qualities of a Phoenix, burn completely to rise as a new woman.

Becoming almost glassy eyed, she continues, "Now let me tell you about the Houston I know. He will do anything to get ahead. His company is his only true love. She is a jealous mistress, believe me. Because of this, he has become a master of deception. The Houston Donovan I know and have known for twenty years is consuming. He makes me forget who I am. I learned if I wanted to be with him, losing my identity is the price I had to pay. He is almost a punishing lover. Taking care of my needs wasn't a question. He always did that. But HD's needs, now that is another story. Let me clarify when I say HD's needs, I'm not referring to Houston Donovan's, but the needs of Highland Diversified. Those are the ones that eventually won out. It's almost as if I am an afterthought."

By the expression, I see you are trying to hide, you understand what I am talking about. Have you realized that his' company's initials are the same as his name? Did he tell you that we called him by his first name until he entered college?"

Sitting listening to her, it's as if I'm paralyzed. My body won't or can't, I'm not sure which, follow the directions my head is giving. Barely, shaking my head, I look at her with a totally shocked face. Finally, managing to say, "I don't want to hear anymore."

"You might not want to hear more but we both know you are going to listen, aren't you? We both know what that burning desire for him is like. Now, you understand that I really do know him." The only motion it seems my body is capable of is nodding in agreement that yes, I would continue to listen.

"I've known him a long time. My brother and Houston were good friends. Their friendship started when they were in second grade. Houston's parents divorced when he was really young, two I think, or maybe he was three. Oh well, doesn't matter. Anyway, Hugh was at the house a lot. His mother was a mess. She would leave him with a nanny/babysitter and be gone for days. So he came to our house. Even when his Mother began moving the men in, he came to us. It was almost as if Houston was my brother. Just like the old saying, my brother but by another mother. The two of them did everything together. They got into lots of trouble but they got away with so much more. I was always the little sister hanging around. They didn't really pay much attention to me. Believe me, I paid attention to them! Ben, the big brother that I worshiped, and his friend, oh yes, I knew all of their secrets. There were many." With a smile, I call almost sinister, she adds "I still know a great many of their dirty little secrets. Secrets that I am sure they both think are long forgotten. Oh, the companies, even a small country or two, I could bring down if I was ever to choose to." With a pifff and a wave of her hand as if she is dismissing the thought, Penny continues, "Like I would want to?" Sitting almost frozen to the sofa, she starts again, "I don't know how much of old grandfather Nigel's story he told you but I want you to think, do you know Houston's full name?"

Slowly shaking my head, she said, "I'm not surprised because he hates it. His full name is Nigel Houston Donovan."

Suddenly, I can feel bile rising in my throat. My eyes are beginning to burn. Blinking rapidly, the only thing I can do is sit. When once before I was almost frozen to the spot, I find that I can't feel my legs even if I did want to escape this horrible horrendous scene.

"You can imagine what kids called him when they found out his first name. Up until he went away to college, we all called him Nigel. His mother still does."

This woman is crazy! I don't know if I can believe one thing she is telling me. Right now, that is not the issue. Houston is the issue. Looking her directly in the eyes, I demand, "Where is he? Tell me the truth." I am beginning to panic. "You just said you stopped him from coming home to me. How did you stop him?" What if this woman has hurt him? You hear about those kinds of things happening. Squaring my shoulders, drawing on my inner strength, I ask, "Did you hurt Houston?"

With a sinister laugh, only one word escapes her ruby red lips, "No."

My only inner question is can I believe this psycho sitting in front of me?

"Sweetie, I did tell you the truth. He went home. I came to see him. A little surprise. I was in town and thought I would drop by to say "hello." He had no time for me!"

"You are lying. You just said you were in town and just dropped by to see Houston. A few minutes ago, you implied you came to Miami to meet me. So which is it?"

Closing her eyes and just barely shaking her head, in a voice dripping with sarcasm, Penny asks "Can't you keep up? I thought you were clever! Back to my story about earlier. He was rushing around talking to Nash. Don't look so shocked. Of course, I know Nash. I know Jeff, also. Unless he has taken on new bodyguards, I know all of them. He was discussing some nonsense about telling someone something. Anyway, he sent Nash on an errand." Pointing to the sofa, "While I sat right there, where you are, he went into his bathroom to shower and change. He left me alone. It was almost as if I didn't exist."

Looking over at his desk, sneering as she speaks, "I walked over to his desk and his cellular device was just lying there. I was shocked. Houston rarely leaves it laying around, as I'm sure you know." Still looking toward his desk, she shrugs and continues, "For some reason, he must have turned off the password protection because when I touched it…"

That term, cellular device, flashes back to me. Somewhere in the back of my mind, I have heard Houston call his phone that. I think it might have been

272

one morning when we were showering. Closing my mind to what this horrible woman is saying, I think back.

Snapping her fingers at me, I heard her continue with this bazaar tale. "It woke up just like that. I've always been a quick thinker. So, I seized the moment. I went to his recent calls and there was your name. Imagine my surprise when it said video chat?"

Sitting there with an indescribable expression, a cross between hatred and pride, she continues. "First, pretending to be Hugh, I sent you a text to come to him. I gather he was going to surprise you by going out in the limo from what I read of his conversation with Jeff. Then, I sent Jeff a text not to pick you up and bring you here. That plans had changed. I told him to take the night off. I ordered that new taxi for you." Smiling an evil smile she continues, "He came out of his bathroom smelling so good, looking so good. I knew he couldn't be here when you arrived. So, I told him you had sent him a text that said you felt bad. That you needed him. You can bet he took off as fast as he could."

Looking at her with all I can muster. I force myself to focus on Penny. "Why are you doing this to me?" I manage to squeak out.

From what I see in her eyes, I am beginning to think this woman is deranged. She says, "I have my reasons. I've always loved him. At first, it was an infatuation as usual with little sisters. He was always around. Then all of a sudden, he wasn't. I didn't find out what happened to their friendship until I was older."

We sat quietly for a minute. "We were celebrating me returning to work, tonight." Suddenly, I feel like it was important for her to know how long we had been together so I randomly blurt out, "We planned on celebrating our six month anniversary, also."

Looking at me as if I have sprouted two heads, Penny repeats me as if she is asking me what I have just said, "Six months? What?"

"I've known Houston six months next week." Sighing, I want her to know, I'm not giving up easily. "I said we have been together six months. Practically from the day we met, we have been together." Now, it's my turn. Reaching up to my neck, I finger the necklace, trying to draw strength from anything I can. Seeing the smug look on her face change to disbelief, I continue.

"I love Houston. Whatever the two of you have "shared" in the past, I would think is over. You just said he acted as if you didn't exist. Well, maybe from his view, you don't. Maybe he doesn't see you as anything other than a bad mistake from his past. You are correct. This might surprise you but I already know he puts Highland Diversified first. What businessman on his level doesn't?" Swallowing hard, I pause to catch my breath. I am on a roll and I will not let this person from his past have the upper hand. She has absolutely no idea who she is dealing with. Continuing on with my tirade, "How could Diversified have grown to be the size it is now, if he didn't? How could he be one of the richest men in America if not the world, if he didn't put it first? You must be delusional if you think otherwise. Any woman, including myself must understand what loving the man that owns a company the size of his means. If you think the tale of woe you have told me tonight scares me, I must admit you are correct it does." Holding up my index finger to prevent her from speaking, I continue, "Here is the thing you don't know, I have been through hell and back in my life. I know what it takes to overcome some of the most horrific things you can imagine. Now, listen to what I am saying, I love Houston Donovan and get this bitch, he loves me."

Finally, stopping, I follow her eyes as they move to something over my head. I glance over my shoulder, and that's when I realize we are no longer alone. Feeling as if a weight has been lifted from me, I know nothing horrible has happened to him.

Turning completely around, my heart is in my throat. He has gone all out tonight for me. He is dressed in a tuxedo. Even in this bizarre scene, any woman with eyes would be melting when they first laid eyes on him. Rising to my feet, I fight the need that I have to rush to him only to feel his powerful arms wrapped around me.

Penny shoots him a quick question, "Houston, what are you doing back here?"

Somehow the way he answers her almost expressionless stops me from moving. "You know exactly what I am doing here, I found out from our doorman, to my surprise that Charli had left in a taxi." Watching him, I notice how his eyes are no longer that yummy brown but black as he speaks. "I wondered why she would do that. That is when I began to put two and two together as they say. I rushed back here because I realized that I left you in my office and that unfortunately, Charli was more than likely with you."

Taking a deep sigh Penny's voice is sugary sweet. "Oh Hugh, I had this all under control. Why did you come back here?" Rolling her eyes she answers her own question but all that sweetness has turned bitterness. "I know you just said you came back for her. Thinking with the wrong head again, Houston? You just can't keep it in your pants, can you? That has always been a problem for you."

Shaking her head, she actually tsks, tsks me. "While you were in the shower, I sent Jeff a text from your phone telling him that his services wouldn't be needed." Pointing at me but keeping her eyes on Houston, she says, "then I sent a taxi for your little love bug here." Still standing in the doorway of his office, I can tell by the dark expression on his face Houston is seething as she opens her mouth to speak.

Cutting her off, he speaks. "Penny, I want you out of this office and my line of sight, right now! I will handle this discussion. This is between Charli and myself."

"Like you have handled the last six months? Come on Houston, six months? She doesn't even know the real reason your paths crossed, does she?" With the fiercest look I have ever seen, he bursts into the room as if he is a Marine storming the enemy but with the roar of a lion, he yells, "NO!"

Not coming to where we are but going to his desk, he jerks open a drawer, removing something. It looks like some type of book. For just a minute I'm not sure who the enemy is, me or her. Looking at him, I begin to realize this isn't the Houston Donovan I know. I've never seen him this angry. As a matter of fact, I am not sure I have ever seen anyone at his level of anger. What I do understand is, he needs to calm down. With this knowledge, I calmly say "Houston."

Turning slowly he looks at me as if it is the first time he had seen me tonight. With a voice as tender as I have ever heard escape from his lips he says, "Charli, we need to have a conversation but it doesn't need to be here. It does need to be between just the two of us." Looking over at the woman across from me he adds, "Only the two of us. You can leave."

"You have got to be kidding? I am not about to miss this little scene. You owe me that much Houston. If you have what I think you do in that book, my suggestion would be for you to put it back." Continuing to hold the book that I now plainly see has some papers sticking out of the side of it he walks away from his desk. I understand this is the emotionless, world dominating Houston not my sexy, passionate Houston. This definitely isn't the same Houston walking to me that has been so kind and loving. The tone of his voice is firm but one I don't recognize.

Penny is right. I don't know this Houston. I'm not sure I want to know this man, either. This is the side of him that he has warned me about. I must admit I didn't want to believe what he said. This is definitely the world domination, Houston. Tipping my head just a little to the left, I am fighting with myself not to gasp as I watch this man walking toward me.

Stopping in front of me, he pulls me to him and kisses me with a fierceness that I have only felt one other time, the night of the vultures. Drawing back from me, I can't help but think that he told me that night that it wasn't always about me. Didn't I know that? Isn't that what I just told Penny. Penny, I forgot she was in the room.

Looking at him searching his eyes for my Houston, he says, "Charli, you are stunning tonight. This obviously is not how I perceived this evening would progress. Kissing me once again, this time tender and gently, all I can think is to hell with her. I melt to him as I feel his strong arms around me. Just as he pulls away, I hear him whisper, "I am sorry for what is about to happen. I ask you no not ask but beg you in advance for forgiveness. Please know that when we began I never meant to hurt you."

Feeling a wave of coldness sweep over me, I look him directly in the eyes saying, "Whatever you have to say to me, just do it here, now. Please, get it over with."

With a curt businesslike nod, instead of guiding me to the door, he takes me by the elbow solemnly walking toward the conference table. I stumble since my legs feel as if they are made from stone. Blinking my eyes, I question if the room is spinning just a little or is it me? I am fearful for what I am suddenly facing. How could this be happening? Three hours ago, I was the happiest woman alive. Now, I don't know what I am. Wrapping his arm around me to help steady me, he mumbles, "be strong, Baby. Be strong." Houston leans across me pulling out one of those cream chairs at the very same table I fantasized about just a little time ago but now seems as if it was light-years ago. Standing here, I take a deep breath as if I am preparing for battle. Maybe I am. I just don't know what type of battle or what will the victor get. Will it be Houston? Is that what I am preparing for? A life with the man I love. Closing my eyes, I sit down. Realizing, this horror isn't a dream.

Opening them, I see the despicable woman sitting across from me. I'm still trying to place where I've seen her. Our eyes are locked in what feels like another battle. A battle, I fear I am loosing. Houston sits down at the head of the table unbuttoning his jacket. At sometime, he has removed his tie and unbuttoned the top button. Even though he is tieless, he looks natural sitting there. As he looks at me first, then at Penny, his facial expression is unreadable. This is the businessman. This is a side of him I have never seen before. I'm not sure I ever want to see it again. Turning to me, businesslike and almost emotionless he speaks.

"I want you to understand, I started this thing between us with one objective. I wanted to get to know you. I wanted to spend time with you. Remember the night at the bar, the smile night? I must admit, I went there with one objective. I knew you would be there or at least there was a strong possibility you would be. I wanted to study your movements. I must admit it was for business purposes. Somewhere along the way, I lost sight of my original objective. I developed true honest feelings for you. The passion we share is real. The love I feel for you is very real. I can no longer think of a future without you."

Sitting in disbelief, I manage to spit out, "Houston, you are scaring me. Please tell me whatever else you think you must say. I can assure you of this, I have no idea why I would have been of interest to you before we met that day."

Continuing in his boardroom manner, he says, "The things you are going to hear will forever change your thoughts of me. I understand that but you must hear them." Looking over at Penny, he says, "I had planned to have this conversation with you but at a time I felt was right. Definitely, I wouldn't have selected tonight but that decision was taken out of my hands."

Pausing for a second, he begins. "Charli, the story I told you is partially true. Remember, when I told you about my name. What it was based upon? How I created a lie? Then, I used that same lie to my advantage?"

Looking at those chocolate eyes, my only response was, "How could I forget that night?" Unconsciously, I found myself reaching up to touch my necklace. I had used that exact same motion to give me comfort several times these past few months. Now, I'm beginning to wonder if the necklace was special at all. At this very minute, I'm not sure what it is.

Continuing he says, "I'm a different man now from the person that originally created that horrible lie. It was almost addictive to create and present the fictitious stories. I twisted the Nigel and Penelope story so many times." Pausing for a minute, he snarls as he continues with the story. " But that is about all that is true about them. I convinced myself that was the way it happened. That Nigel was sent away from his family. That he was disowned."

Finding my courage to speak, "We have all made mistakes. You were younger. What I want to know the most is, how many women have you told the story to, Houston?"

Ignoring me, he continues, "My Great, Great, Grandfather was named Nigel Houston. He did come here from Scotland. However, he came here of his own free will. He was from a wealthy family but he was headstrong and wanted to create his own empire. he did meet Penelope here in the United States." Exhaling deeply he finishes, "Unfortunately, the majority of the tale wasn't based on him. With a few exceptions here and there, it is actually based on me, my past. " Looking me directly in the eye, he continues, "It was just a mere coincidence that she shares a similar name," as he points to the evil woman that is sitting directly across from me. "I have no doubt Penny has shared my full name during her time with you. So you see, it was about a Nigel Houston just not the one I implied."

Attempting to swallow, I fear that even my saliva won't go down. I simply know my throat is closing. Finding the courage to continue, I ask again, "How many women, Houston. How many?"

"Baby, do you really want to know?"

That does it. I just found my fight, "Don't you dare Baby me, Houston Donovan! The story wasn't just for one woman. How many?"

Shaking his head, he finally answers my question. "Charli, I actually don't know. I've lost count. I have told that same story so many times." We sit here, as I process what he has just conveyed to me. I believed him. He was so convincing.

Dropping my head, I sit staring at my clasp hands in my lap. Raising my head, I look the man who is destroying my future and I ask, "So you are a consummate liar, then?"

Penny's laugh, when I voice that question, makes my skin crawl. I would like to lean across the table and claw her eyes out. Shifting my eyes from Houston to Penny and back again to Houston, I am afraid to ask the question, I know I have to ask. Directing him to look at me, I reach out at a snail's pace to touch him on the arm. Hesitating, it is almost as if I am afraid touching him will burn me. No matter what my mind says, my body longs for contact with him. Even the feel of him through his jacket sleeve is better than nothing. As our eyes meet, I find the courage to voice the one question that will more than likely change my life forever, "Houston, who is she?"

Penny begins to answer, I jerk my head around and look her in the eye, pointing at her with as much of a sneering voice as I can muster I fling the words at her, "I have heard enough from you. I want to hear it from Houston."

Turning back to him, I watch as he opens his mouth to answer, then changes his mind. I have never seen him at a loss for words. His face has an unreadable expression. He lowers his head just a little, but not in shame. When he raises it, he rubs his hand across his forehead. I realize, he is forming the words in his head, first. Sitting quietly, just waiting what seems like an eternity, finally he looks me in the eye and says,

"She's my wife."

Looking at Houston, I manage to mumble, "Your wife? You are not married."

With a light in her eyes that causes her face to take on a look of someone possessed, Penny leans over, removing my hand from Houston's arm, "Yes, he is you marriage wrecking whore. He's married to me."

Barley, above a whisper I say, "If the story is about you then...Penelope is actually?" I look across the table at Penny and back to Houston. The bile that was rising earlier is now, in my throat. I swallow hard to keep it down. I point to each of them as I speak, "Nigel and Penelope?"

Drawing in deeply, he replies in the coldest, calmest, scariest tone of voice I think I have ever heard. "I said earlier that Nigel and Penelope were my great, great grandparents, which is true. Penny's name is just that Penny."

It feels as if my body is moving in slow motion, but somehow I make it to my feet. Barely able to cross the room, I say nothing. The silence that has engulfed the room says it all. What is there to say? Besides, making a sound, much less forming words into any type of understandable speech, isn't something I am really capable of at this moment. Stopping in the doorway where the man, I believed loved me, stood only moments ago, I turn to look at him one final time. I want something other than that bitch removing my hand from him as my last visual of Houston Donovan. No, not want, I need to store a different memory into my brain than what is floating around in my head at this moment. Standing here, I am drinking in the sight of the man I love but can never have. Looking at him sitting at that table, I realize why she looks familiar. I feel as if I will be sick. She was the red head at his table the night we met. Trying to forget that, I focus on Houston. All I can see is the world dominating businessman sitting at the head of his conference table. This version of him has replaced my Houston. Both have that irresistible lock, falling across his forehead. The one that I've felt touch me so many times when he was

285

kissing my neck's special spot. The tightening of his fists seems to match the speed in which he is clenching his jaw. Penny opens her mouth. I squint my eyes and shake my head. She understands that at this moment, the thing for her to do is to remain silent. Houston looks at me with those glorious chocolate eyes, a pain seems to be etched into his face that mirrors my own, I'm sure. Neither of us wanting to break what in all probability will be our final connection, he says, "I will always love you."

Hearing this, I know without a doubt I am destroyed. Drawing on what little remaining strength that can possibly be hiding deep inside, I turn and leave his office. Exiting the building is difficult, but leaving Houston sitting with her encases my body in an almost unbearable agony. Leaving him is more than difficult. It ranks as being one of the most agonizing things I have ever endured. Throughout everything, I have survived in my brief thirty-two years, even situations some would call horrific, I have always remained hopeful. At this moment, any and all hope for a future with him is gone. The heart wrenching information that was hurled around upstairs has left me crushed. Stopping on the sidewalk, to compose myself, I close my eyes and breathe deeply trying to remain as calm as possible because I refuse to fall apart here. Turning, I tilt my head back, look up at the top floor. I have no idea how long I stand just looking. Finally, realizing my surroundings it occurs to me that I should remove myself from here. My feet and brain are not communicating. It is as if I can't pull myself away from the building. The thought of walking away leaving him up there with her causes me to realize I have no claim to the man I truly love. Try telling that to my shattered heart.

As a reader myself, I understand there are thousands of books for you to select from. Thank you for selecting Shattered Heart, The Charli Jensen Story. This is the first in the series, Life's Second Chances. It is my greatest hope that you enjoyed my first attempt at writing. If you did enjoy Charli's story, I would greatly appreciate you supporting my writing endeavors by leaving a positive review. Thanks again!

Happy Reading,
Carol

Besides my author page, please visit my website at
carolmaybooks.com
Follow me on Twitter
http://twitter.com/carolmaybooks
Friend me on Facebook

Turn the page for an excerpt from. Book Two in the Life's Second Chances series featuring Charli Jensen.

Love, Lies and Shattered Hearts

Chapter 1
Charli

"NO! You are wrong. He isn't dead." I shout.

My eyes dart around the room searching for any possible way to escape from this medical prison. The average person would say I am lucky to be in this ICU room. The seat belt failed I was ejected. That is the only reason I am alive. These blue-tan walls are a constant reminder of just how *lucky* I am. "I know he is somewhere in this hospital. Just let me see him. You are wrong! Let me out of this bed!" I yell as I try to move my hands but these black cuffs won't let me. I have asked every person that enters this room if he is really dead. They all have said to me in one way or another, "Honey, I am so sorry but yes he is."

I still can't believe that I am wrong. He died. I try to get up but all of these wires, are tying me down. Looking up into a face that is not much older than mine I beg, "Please, tell me the truth. Please." Tears are streaming down my face in rivers that mirror the sorrow I feel.

"Ms. Jensen, please lay down and try to get some rest," she says wiping the tears from my eyes since I can't raise my hands.

Anyone within hearing distance of this room knows I'm alive. They can hear my heart racing a million miles an hour because of that damn monitor hovering above my head. Closing my eyes, I mumble to the room, "Isn't there a volume control?" It's going crazy. Beep, beep, beep. I don't want to hear it. It is a reminder that I am alive and he is not. When something is broken it isn't suppose to work. My heart is broken. Why is it working?

"No sir, I'm afraid she isn't awake now." That's what she thinks, I can hear every word that evil person in blue is saying. I simply can't find the energy to open my eyes. Lying here listening to her discuss me in a cold unfeeling voice, as if I am some type of object, not a woman that is wounded. My wounds extend deeper than my physical body. My soul is wounded my heart that houses the love I once had is shattered.

"Sir, I am very sorry to report that she has been combative again today. Her restraints had been removed sometime before my arrival, unfortunately she has tried to pull out her IV's more than once. The doctor decided she must remain restrained until she stops pulling them out. Please forgive me for saying so, she certainly is strong willed. Yes, Sir I know it must be difficult for you to be there. Each time the sedative wears off, the fighting to get up and the yelling begins. Yes, when she is awake, she is in quite a bit of pain. She refuses to accept the truth."

Their voices are getting further and further away. I can't hear … We're walking on the beach. I'm laughing at the playfulness we are caught up in. It's as if nothing can touch us. I stop to look in the clear shallow water at the shells that are being washed ashore. Bending over, I try to pick up a brightly colored one but my arms are like rubber. Suddenly the water is a light shade of pink. Pulling my hand back, I see it is bleeding. The blood is running down my arm in a steady stream. I can't see where it is coming from.

I am half lying on top of something hard. Struggling to open my eyes, I find that the air around me is filled with a thick, gray smoke that burns them, causing me close them immediately. I have no idea where I am or the reason I can't move. Somewhere off in the distance, I hear someone. Whoever it is, they sound very far away. That loud popping sound makes it difficult to hear. I can barely make out that it is a man's voice. Through the moans I hear a faint, "Help."